DANCEFLOOR

CW01395680

DANCEFLOOR

VICTOR JESTIN

Translated from the French by Sam Taylor

SCRIBNER

London · New York · Amsterdam/Antwerp · Sydney/Melbourne · Toronto · New Delhi

First published in Great Britain by Scribner,
an imprint of Simon & Schuster UK Ltd, 2025

Copyright © 2025 Victor Jestin
Translation copyright Samuel Taylor © 2025
First published in French as *L'homme qui danse*, Flammarion, 2022

SCRIBNER and design are registered trademarks of The Gale Group, Inc.,
used under licence by Simon & Schuster Inc.

The right of Victor Jestin to be identified as author of this work has been asserted
in accordance with the Copyright, Designs and Patents Act, 1988.

1 3 5 7 9 10 8 6 4 2

Simon & Schuster UK Ltd, 1st Floor
222 Gray's Inn Road, London WC1X 8HB

For more than 100 years, Simon & Schuster has championed authors and the
stories they create. By respecting the copyright of an author's intellectual property,
you enable Simon & Schuster and the author to continue publishing exceptional
books for years to come. We thank you for supporting the author's copyright
by purchasing an authorized edition of this book.

No amount of this book may be reproduced or stored in any format, nor may it
be uploaded to any website, database, language-learning model, or other repository,
retrieval, or artificial intelligence system without express permission. All rights
reserved. Inquiries may be directed to Simon & Schuster, 222 Gray's Inn Road,
London WC1X 8HB or RightsMailbox@simonandschuster.co.uk

Simon & Schuster Australia, Sydney
Simon & Schuster India, New Delhi

www.simonandschuster.co.uk
www.simonandschuster.com.au
www.simonandschuster.co.in

A CIP catalogue record for this book is available from the British Library

The authorised representative in the EEA is Simon & Schuster Netherlands BV,
Herculesplein 96, 3584 AA Utrecht, Netherlands. info@simonandschuster.nl

Simon & Schuster strongly believes in freedom of expression and stands against
censorship in all its forms. For more information, visit BooksBelong.com.

Trade Paperback ISBN: 978-1-3985-3169-7
eBook ISBN: 978-1-3985-3170-3
eAudio ISBN: 978-1-3985-3171-0

This book is a work of fiction. Names, characters, places and incidents are either
a product of the author's imagination or are used fictitiously. Any resemblance
to actual people living or dead, events or locales is entirely coincidental.

Printed and Bound in the UK using 100% Renewable Electricity at CPI Group (UK) Ltd

MIX
Paper | Supporting
responsible forestry
FSC
www.fsc.org FSC® C013604

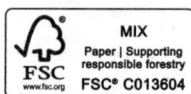

'I would love to love to love.'

FERNANDO PESSOA,
Fragments of a Motionless Journey

At daybreak, nightclubs betray us. In an instant they reveal their ugliness and squalor. The lights come on, the music falls silent. The air smells like the inside of a sweatshop. The floor sticks to our soles, and the palm tree is revealed as plastic. We see that there are walls and a ceiling, a room with ordinary dimensions. Worst of all, everyone leaves. Only the drunkest and the most desperate remain, like children refusing to go to bed. The bouncers shove them outside. The party is over. All that's left is the empty building – and me, forgotten in a booth at the back of the club.

My eyes sting from the tears I've shed. My head feels hot. I lie on my side, my face resting on leather. I don't know what time it was when I fell asleep. It must have been sad, but funny too. I am almost forty. For this place, that's old; it's practically dead. I am past my sell-by date. It's time to leave. But I don't know where to go.

I can hear the barman washing glasses, but he can't see me.

Everything's all right. I still have time. In fact, if I squint at the dancefloor, I can even imagine that it's filled with people, a whole crowd of them dancing the night away, at least for a little while longer.

GUY

1990

The first time I came here, I was ten years old.

I remember, I was sitting on the bench in the school play-ground, feet dangling, alone like someone on their first day. But it wasn't my first day: I had been at that same school, with those same kids, since I was six. The other boys were playing football a few feet from where I sat. I watched them, smiling, hoping that they'd let me play.

That was when Anthony came over.

'I'm having my birthday party on Sunday in a special place. We need to have as many boys as girls, and one of the boys can't come. Do you want to take his place?'

I was touched by his invitation.

'Okay.'

He gave me a blue envelope, then went back to his football match.

*

My parents weren't used to taking me to other children's birthday parties. I'd been to a few, but the invitations always came from family friends or from neighbours. Anthony's party was different – it was the real deal. When I showed them the envelope, they congratulated me as though it was my birthday.

At five o'clock on Sunday afternoon, we went to the rendezvous point. It was a car park with a yellow rectangular building at it its centre, like a giant shipping container. The other guests were waiting outside. Anthony's uncle welcomed us. His name was Guy. A tanned, muscular, blond guy, he looked like he ought to be a swimming instructor or an activity leader at a summer camp. He proudly explained that the building was called The Beach and that he was the owner. He said it was a 'nightclub'. I didn't know what that meant. My parents, on the other hand, looked worried. They asked me if I was really okay with this. I didn't want to make trouble, so I said yes, and they left me with Guy, who told me to join the others. I knew most of them; they were in my class. I was about to say hello to them, but Guy clapped his hands.

'All right, you little monsters, you wanna see what it's like inside?'

Everyone yelled: 'Yeah!' I said it too, more quietly, and we went in.

We walked in line through a dark corridor. It smelled of paint and dust, as though they hadn't finished doing it up. Guy opened another door and we came out into a vast empty room, the kind of place where people play basketball at a recreation centre, illuminated by fluorescent lights. There were some tables and chairs along the walls, like they'd been pushed there to make space for something to happen.

'You wanna dance?!'

Everyone yelled: 'Yeah!' I wanted to say it too, but this time no sound came out. After that, it was all too much for me. Guy sat at a table, on top of which there was a machine with electric wires trailing from it. He pressed a button and the lights went out, replaced by a multicoloured mirrorball that hung from the ceiling. Suddenly, there was a tension in the air. We all looked more beautiful.

'Boys over here, girls over there. When I start the music, boys, you have to ask a girl to dance!'

The two groups lined up. I was taken aback, but I got in line too. Within a few seconds, I found myself facing the girls, separated from them and then instantly ordered to join them.

Madonna – 'Like A Prayer'

Nobody moved.

'Come on boys, you can do it!'

Anthony was the first to make up his mind. He walked across the dancefloor towards a girl. The others followed, and a series of couples formed. The music grew louder, and in the same instant, as if this was something they'd rehearsed, they all started to dance. Their arms and legs began making strange, inventive movements, and pairs of children twirled across the floor, which suddenly seemed to be moving too, criss-crossed by circles of light. I found myself alone – except for the fact that, facing me, stood a girl who was even more alone. Aurélie, the last one standing. She had kept her sweater on over her knee-length dress, out of which poked a pair of spindly legs, making her look like a pink flamingo. She stared at me fearfully. Was she afraid that I would ask her to dance, or that I would not ask her to dance?

'Come on, you're the last one!' Guy shouted at me.

I wanted to move forward, but I couldn't. The floor felt like mud. I was stuck to it. I tried several times, summoning all my strength, all my determination, but each time something inside pulled me back, as if I was standing at the edge of a diving board.

Guy left the table and came over to me. The music went on without him, and the others kept dancing. Everything appeared automatic.

'What's up, Arthur? You don't want to dance?'

'It's not that . . .'

'She's not your type?'

'It's not that . . .'

'Are you scared about the others seeing you?'

'It's not that . . .'

'So what is it, then?'

I tried to find the words to explain it to him.

'I can't move.'

'Sure you can.'

'No, really, I can't.'

'Give me your hand.'

He took my hand and led me towards Aurélie. I felt my shoes scraping against the floor, as if I was a wardrobe being dragged. And yet I was walking, putting one foot in front of the other.

'See? You can move.'

He let go of me. I was standing in front of Aurélie.

'Now ask her to dance.'

She stared at her shoes and I stared at mine.

'Ask her. You can see she's embarrassed.'

I could see this and I felt bad. I had nothing against her. In other circumstances, I would have been happy to get to know her. It was simply that I couldn't dance.

But I had to. The others were watching. I felt shame subsuming me. I was being rude. I was ruining the party. They wouldn't invite me again.

I managed to raise my hand and hold it for a few seconds at waist height between Aurélie and me. Suddenly she grabbed it. I put my arm around her back. We clung to each other.

'And now dance with her.'

I didn't know how. Nobody had ever shown me. I needed something to set me off. Every idea of movement carried within it all the other ideas that first had to be rejected. I tried several times, but I was like a stalled car. My efforts were invisible. An outside observer would probably have concluded that I was simply refusing.

'Come on, it's not difficult! Just let yourself go – watch!'

And Guy began to dance, lifting his thighs one after another, snapping his fingers and smiling. I thought he was ugly. He wanted me to dance; he was obsessed by the idea. What would happen if I continued to disobey him? Would he start yelling? I should burst into tears, I thought. That was the only way I could make him understand. The only way I would ever be left in peace. But I couldn't make myself cry. I was too angry.

I let go of Aurélie's hand.

'All right, that's enough,' sighed Guy. 'This is a nightclub – it's for dancing. Can you imagine what would happen if everyone acted like you? Come on, dance with me – I'll show you how it's done.'

He grabbed hold of my hand. Suddenly I cried out: 'No!' And I slapped his hand with my free hand. It made a loud noise. I looked at him, gritting my teeth, certain that he was about to start shouting at me. Instead, he slapped my face. He slapped it so hard that it made an even louder noise and my cheek burned. The tears came at last. Guy put his head in his hands and groaned. The others had all frozen. Only the music and lights continued, as if whispering insistently: Come on, Arthur, just take one step and the rest will follow …

VINCENT

1998

The next time was eight years later.

'Hey, let's go to a club!'

I was smoking on Vincent's sofa, next to two other boys who I don't remember – extras. I do remember Vincent, though. He was a big guy and he would always wear white T-shirts and dirty jeans. Sometimes his body odour was overpowering, but even that worked in his favour, giving the impression – along with all his movements – that he was mature for his age, a man among boys. He was right-handed but he held his cigarette in his left hand. I liked the way he would rummage in his pocket for his lighter, a cigarette dangling from his mouth, then tilt his head to light it; the way he would punctuate his phrases by taking a long drag that left us hanging on his next word; the way he would toss his dog-end away to indicate that the conversation was over. Sitting beside him, half my arse hanging over the edge of the sofa, I concentrated on inhaling the smoke deeply, the way

I'd practiced in my bedroom. I was hoping I would enjoy it a bit – just a bit, so that he would see it on my face – but it tasted foul, like dust and death, and the smoke burned my throat so badly that it brought tears to my eyes. I said I was allergic to the sofa. I would have done anything to stay there, in that collective cloud of smoke, to make time stand still. The truth was, I wasn't really their friend at all. I was just a hanger-on, a parasite, who had slowly insinuated himself into the group, worn them down over time; the kind of friend whose presence or absence was equally negligible.

'Come on, let's go to a club,' Vincent repeated.

I continued to pretend that I hadn't heard him, waiting for the others to say no in my place.

'Why do you want to go to a club?'

'I'm bored of staying here every night. I prefer it when there are loads of people.'

'They won't let us in.'

'Yeah they will! I've been with my brother's mates before. They didn't even check my ID card.'

'I don't want to dance, anyway.'

'So? Me neither. Who gives a shit about dancing? You don't dance for the sake of dancing – you dance because you're on the pull.'

On the pull: that phrase made me feel sick. In their language, it meant trying to kiss a girl. They'd been obsessed with this idea for a while. It had happened slowly since we started secondary school together: their bodies had thickened, their voices had deepened, and they had started, little by little, to stare more fixedly at girls, their gazes descending in a single movement over breasts and legs and *arses*, as they called them – a word that made me blush whenever I repeated it. I wasn't ready for this. I still looked like a little kid.

'Come on!' Vincent urged us. 'I reckon even Arthur could pull there.'

The others laughed, and so did I, my face muscles tensed. Vincent always wanted me to pull. Every time we went out, he would try to find someone for me. For him it counted as a good deed, a humanitarian act of charity. I had never kissed a girl – not even a quick peck on the lips or a snog in the corner of the playground – and that fact bothered him. While the others were already dreaming about having sex, I was still stuck waiting to get to first base. I would really have to do it one day, if only to stop them laughing at me.

'I'm up for it,' I said suddenly, with a jolt of courage.

Before we set off, the other two must have phoned home to ask their parents' permission. They envied me and Vincent because we had more freedom than they did. Our parents never told us we couldn't go out, albeit for different reasons: his because they generally weren't around; mine because any hint of socialisation was a good sign, a small victory over my solitude.

There wasn't much happening in the town centre at that time of night: a few bars were still open, along with our favourite corner shop; the night bus moved quietly through the empty streets; and there was a kebab place, where we would end up in the early morning. And then, on the other side of the Loire, before you reached the industrial zone, there was The

Beach, the only nightclub in town, a bright yellow cuboid on the docks. I never went to that part of town. As we got closer, something made my stomach lurch – and it wasn't just the bass booming through the walls. As soon as I saw the building, I recognised it, and all my anxiety came rushing back, like when you turn a corner and you're startled by the memory of a particular geometry or the pain of an old humiliation.

We crossed the bridge and walked through the car park to the entrance. Big neon letters on the building's façade spelled out 'The Beach'. Several people were waiting in line. We stood behind them. I pretended I was fine. Maybe the others were pretending too, but they were doing a better job of it than me. Everyone else in the queue appeared to be adults in their twenties. When it was our turn to go in, the bouncer looked at me. I was afraid he would turn us away and that it would be my fault. Because I was not desirable enough, or perhaps because I didn't have enough desire. Whatever. I stood up straight. I thought about doing something antisocial – spitting on the ground, for example – so that he would reject us for that reason and not because I looked like a virgin.

'Go ahead.'

We were in. Vincent and the others celebrated like they'd just robbed a bank. In the corridor – like an airlock between the outside world and the club itself – the music throbbed louder and I felt as if we were moving slowly deeper under-ground. I thought about other airlocks I had known: the space between the showers and the swimming pool; the queue for a ride at an amusement park; the waiting room for a doctor's office … all of them antechambers of anxiety. Automatically my heart started to race and I kept my arms crossed high on my chest to muffle the pounding. We had left our coats in the cloakroom. They'd given each of us a token. As the corridor narrowed, I had the sudden sensation that we were entering a factory: that we were going not to a place of dancing and alcohol, but to work amidst the stench of coal dust.

Daft Punk – 'Around the World'

Inside, there was a bar, a fake palm tree, a mirrored wall, some purple leather booths in the corners. And, occupying the centre of the room, a rectangular dancefloor where hundreds of people were jerking and twitching in a chaos of music, colours and dry ice. At first I felt as if I was glimpsing movement – something that was changing moment by moment – but that did not last long. Soon what I saw struck me as uniform and permanent. After the first few steps, we were swallowed whole by the atmosphere, drawn in by the lights. Our T-shirts, shoes and teeth started to shine the way they did at the bowling alley. I felt a thrill of excitement pass through the others. They said things that I couldn't hear, because the music was too loud. We went around the dancefloor to the bar. I could tell from the way he walked that Vincent was enjoying the fact of not dancing yet, delaying the moment as confident people do. I tried to mimic him. As long as I wasn't dancing, there was nothing to prove that I wasn't a great dancer, a womaniser who brilliantly hid his intentions behind the mask of a shy daydreamer.

'Four whisky and cokes!' Vincent yelled at the barman, without asking us what we wanted. He slapped a hundred-franc note on the counter.

I would never have dared order drinks for everyone. It was like getting up first to leave the cafeteria – only leaders knew how to do that. I didn't know what a whisky and coke was, and I would have preferred just a coke, or at most a Malibu, but I didn't say anything. Afterwards I followed the others to the booths, holding my glass high and concentrating on it – my excuse for not dancing. Some alcohol spilled on my sleeve. We sat in a row at the edge of the dancefloor. I had never seen so many people moving around in a single room before. I looked up at the ceiling, so I wouldn't have to watch them, and saw dozens of spotlights whirling around at an infernal speed, each a different colour and following a different trajectory, all of them playing their part in the chaos. They looked exhausted, as though they were struggling to keep spinning. I lowered my eyes and focused on the music. I felt an urge to tap my foot as if I was at a concert – the kind of laidback concert where everyone remained seated. I would have liked that. Beside me, the other three were having a conversation, yelling in each other's ears. I thought I heard Vincent telling them about a party he'd been to the previous weekend. This was his favourite subject. Even more than going out, he liked talking about going out. For him, the pleasure of a night on the town depended on the story he would be able to tell about it afterwards. He always exaggerated things. The others listened, laughing even before the punchlines came, so eager were they to be amused. I twisted my neck to join in, trying to insert myself into the triangle formed by their bodies, but I couldn't manage it. Their shoulders muscled me out, without even meaning to. I laughed randomly, but it came out too

high-pitched and they didn't hear me. With a sigh, I stared at
the floor and drank my whisky and coke. It was whisky with
Schweppes tonic. Very bitter. It made me gassy. *What the hell
am I doing here?* I thought briefly.

Vincent stood up. He took a few steps forward then started
dancing, his hips swaying, his lips pressed tightly together,
his arms swinging languidly beside his body, as if he was
jogging in slow motion. He moved towards the centre of the
dancefloor, disappearing into the crowd.

'Fucking hell, he can dance!'

'He's good too, that bastard!'

They followed him like flies.

'I'm gonna finish my drink and then I'll join you!' I shouted.

Suddenly the booth in which I was sitting seemed too big.
I sucked the rest of my drink through the straw, making a
horrible slurping noise. I lit a cigarette. Another few minutes
and then I'd dance, I decided. The dancefloor stretched out
like a sea at my feet. There would be girls there that I could
chat up. It was just like an old-fashioned ball, I realised. The
people here weren't waltzing, but the set-up was equally ar-
chaic and cruel. Everyone was looking for a partner. Any time
there was an odd number of dancers, one of us would end up
alone. And there was a very good chance that the odd one out
would be me, just as it was when I used to play musical chairs
as a kid. The people on the dancefloor were pressed together.
They all looked alike. In that light, they blurred into one, the
colours smoothing their faces, erasing their zits, altering their
bodies. The atmosphere was exciting, and dangerous too,
because with all these people becoming more beautiful, the

expectation was intensified, saturating the club with desire, more desire than it could hold. No doubt there was, somewhere, a switch that would turn on the fluorescent ceiling lights, startling the crowd below, making everyone wake up suddenly in the arms of some red, sweating stranger.

I had to dance. If not, it seemed possible I could sit there for hours, for days, without anyone ever coming to find me. I had to try, even if it meant courting disaster. I stood up. The boundary of the dancefloor was not clearly delineated: there was no illuminated groove or change of colour. The only marker was the edge of the crowd itself: the dance zone began with the first moving body. There was a no man's land about five or six feet wide between that body and me. I crossed it, one step after another, walking as carefully as if the floor was ice. I made it into the mass of bodies. Suddenly I felt compelled to think about every part of my body. Even the most banal parts, like my fingers, my feet and my ears, had to be assigned some specific task. How could I dance? How could I set myself in motion? I was paralysed. The seconds passed and I saw people staring at me. I started to panic. The only alternative, if I wanted to avoid humiliation, was to make a show of heading towards a particular destination – any destination – a tactic I had used before, in the school playground. I began walking determinedly towards the bar. I went around the outside most of the way, but at one point, to avoid hitting the wall, I had to turn and cut across the dancefloor. I snaked between bodies. All the different odours mingled into a single, standardised stink of sweat. I became aware of the silence: the bodies were dancing, sometimes touching, but they made no noise. Nobody spoke in this club. Mouths remained shut, secretly salivating, opening only to drink or kiss. All of this went on below the music. There must be another switch, I thought, to turn off the sound, returning everyone to their own silence, to the rustling of their jeans and their breathing in the dark.

When I reached the bar, I put my elbows on the counter, but it was sticky. The barman leaned towards me.

'What do you want?'

'A glass of water, please!'

The alcohol was starting to affect me, and I didn't like that sensation. I had never been able to get serenely drunk, to accept the intoxication, to surrender my control over the situation. I sat on a bar stool, my back to the crowd, and drank my iced water. I had no idea where Vincent and the others were. It was every man for himself. There was a guy near me at the bar, dozing with his elbows on the counter, his head in his hands. He looked old, almost my father's age. He looked as though he'd come to the wrong place. I felt a little bit sorry for him. Nobody was paying him any notice. The two of us were on the sidelines, marginalised. The dancing pulsed outwards from the centre of the floor, pushing its unwanted waste in concentric circles to the corners of the room, the bar, the booths, and ultimately outside. From here, I could tell that the club was not the vast open communal space it appeared to be. It was a hierarchy of different zones, their boundaries blurred by darkness and music. The privileged ones, like Vincent, were not aware of this and moved freely from one zone to another, but some of us stumbled when we came to certain passages, as if there was a step missing; we froze, too scared to dance, then scurried back to our allotted spot. This was not unjust; it was merely a facet of injustice. Injustice itself was bigger, broader: it took in the streets, the corridors of our high school; it spread through the town and far, far beyond. Why would The Beach be any different?

I felt a sudden need to piss. At last I had something to do, something clear and precise. I walked along the wall, searching for the bathroom, before finally finding a small staircase marked by a sign. At the bottom of the steps, the swing door banged violently shut behind me, insulating me from the music, although I could still hear the bass. The stark white light revealed the ugliness of the place: the grimy floor; the slow, heavy bodies, in a rush to get back to the dancefloor. I saw a drunk girl go into a cubicle and sit on the toilet seat without wiping it, her buttocks touching the filth as if nothing could disgust her anymore, so carried away was she by the stubborn desire to mix with others. I hid in a corner and took my time.

'Come for a piss, eh?'

Vincent, sweating and grinning, stood at the urinal next to mine.

'Having a good time?'

'Not bad.'

'Have you pulled?'

'No. Not yet. I'm ... checking them out, you know.'

'Oh yeah? Well, check this out!'

Turning in my direction, he roared loudly and shook his dick at me. I laughed. Vincent was proud of his dick. It was a long and thick. He had been showing it off to me like this for years. The first time I saw it, I had been twelve. We'd been at his house, watching TV, when he'd said: 'Let's wank!' I had replied: 'Sure, why not?' He'd balanced a cushion between us: a mere formality, I assumed, since either of us could have seen the other just by peering over the top. For an instant, I had seen his erection, covered with hair and veins. Vincent had grabbed a handful of tissues, and I'd asked him why. 'For the cum.' I had blushed: I didn't have any. Every night, I would masturbate, praying that it would spurt out at last, but my orgasms were always dry: no white stuff, no proof. Vincent had groaned as he came. He had showed me his tissue afterwards, like the head of a decapitated enemy. When he'd stood up to throw it in the bin, I'd spat in mine before holding it out to him. 'You call that cum?' he'd asked. I'd sworn that it was and he'd laughed. Ever since that day, he kept showing me his dick, and sometimes I would show him mine too, because with Vincent it was important to display your lust, to present it like an ID card at every checkpoint. You had to get hard-ons. You had to swagger and laugh, talk loudly in the street, ogle girls' arses, say the word *arse*, give it the big I Am. He zipped up his jeans.

'I'm going back. I reckon I'm about to pull.'

He left without washing his hands. Standing in front of the mirror, I observed myself. I wasn't ugly or handsome. My features were too angular, my body too tall and skinny, my head bent forward as if inviting someone to chop it off. My shirt looked like the sail of a yacht. My jeans were too baggy: you could see the gap between the denim and my scrawny thighs. My shoes were fine. So there you go . . . I was average. I absolutely understood why no girls were attracted to me. All the same, though, I had to try. One more time. *Come on, Arthur. You'll be glad when you've done it.*

I went back into the mass of bodies, like a soldier going to war. Nothing had changed – even the music seemed the same – and yet a vast amount of work had been done in the shadows, whole minutes of stalking and flirting, the progress barely visible unless you were to bend close to the bodies and count the new couples, the about-to-be couples, the ones who were absent, and all the others who were still on their own. I slipped between them without thinking. I started tapping my foot, and for the moment that seemed enough to justify my presence on the dancefloor. This time I forced myself to look at girls, not to lower my eyes. They all appeared older, more mature than me. They wouldn't even consider me, I thought. I'd be like a kid in their arms. All the same, I spotted a small group of girls who didn't look much older than me, maybe eighteen. It was a question of making eye contact – with any of them – and then walking over, touching, kissing. How complicated could it be? Did I have bad breath? Probably. I had been silent for a long time, my tongue marinating in whisky and saliva. I took a stick of chewing gum from my pocket and tossed it in my mouth while pretending to yawn. No, I really did yawn. I was tired. I didn't feel like doing this. I lacked the energy to force a kiss from the night just so I could show it off to my friends. I needed more calmness, more time. I wished I knew who had made it a rule that desire had to be expressed only at nighttime, amidst alcohol and agitation. I would have preferred the peacefulness of an afternoon. Oh well. I went back to sit in the booth.

A few moments later, a familiar face appeared among the crowd. Amandine, a girl from my class, was dancing by herself in an unassuming way, as if apologising for being there. I watched her. I'd always liked her. I often tried to sit next to her in class. Her presence warmed my heart and gave a sort of meaning to my days. I felt a spark of courage. Now was my chance.

'Fuck, I need to sit down!'

Vincent collapsed beside me in the booth, his arms outstretched along the top of the leather bench, his legs spread wide. He was drunk. I wished he would go away.

'I pulled!' he yelled in my ear. 'But she wouldn't go all the way. I need to find a girl who actually wants to fuck! One of the desperate ones, you know? That's the secret . . . You should pick a girl who's got something wrong with her, like a long nose or sticky-out ears. Something that gives her a complex. If you can handle that, you're in! And you know what they say: nobody looks at the mantelpiece when they're poking the fire!' He roared with laughter, then elbowed me in the ribs. 'Look, that fat cow Amandine is here. I fancy my chances with her . . .'

A second later, he was up on his feet and heading towards her, his hand held out. Surprised, she latched onto it like a piece of driftwood in the sea. My bitterness quickly gave way to a clear-eyed resignation: it was only natural that I should fail before I even tried, so what was the point in feeling jealous? Sitting only about ten feet away, I watched them dance together. Vincent was a good dancer. He was so confident in his abilities, so sure that he was being generous by dancing with Amandine, that he could get away with doing rock moves to a techno track. As for Amandine, she followed his lead, gazing up at him, her face frozen in an expression of fascination and an appreciation of how lucky she was. The track ended and a new song started, almost a ballad. I didn't know people still danced to songs like that. The whole club seemed to slow down in that moment. It was beautiful. Smiling wolfishly, his eyelids lowered, Vincent leaned down to kiss Amandine. They embraced for a long time, her hands on his waist, his hands sliding down her back to fondle her arse and pulling her into his body: his non-negotiable condition if she wanted to keep dancing with him. After a while, he turned to wink at me and I responded with a happy, knowing, self-hating grin. I wanted to leave then. Why shouldn't I? I could even slip out without saying goodbye, but I knew Vincent would slag me off for it afterwards. I took a deep breath, then walked over to them, stiff-backed amidst the swaying crowd.

'Listen, I'm sorry but I'm really tired, so I'm gonna go home now.'

He continued snogging her but gave me the thumbs up behind her back. I didn't dare look at her. I left, crossing the dancefloor one last time, and I noticed that I was no longer afraid of it now that I knew I was on my way out. I even took a sort of pleasure in walking away slowly, the way I used to as a kid in the playground when the bell rang for the end of the school day. Before going through the exit door, I glanced over my shoulder. The party was still raging, indifferent to my departure. It would have been nice if someone had tried to persuade me to stay, or if all the others had gone home at the same time. I went into the dark corridor and picked up my coat from the cloakroom, leaving the others' coats hanging either side of an empty space.

Going outside and breathing fresh air had the same effect on me as putting my shoes back on after an hour at the ice rink: the ground too present under my feet, a heavy feeling in my legs, the slowing down of time, and then – little by little – the simple pleasure of walking unencumbered. The bouncer offered to stamp my forearm in case I wanted to come back later that night. I shook my head – I wasn't planning to return. All the same, as I walked away, I felt a twinge of sadness at the idea that I had, once again, chickened out.

On the docks, some prostitutes stood leaning against a wall, all of them looking alike in their zipped-up puffer jackets and their long black-tighted legs. They whistled at me as I went past. I felt embarrassed, but quite pleased that they at least considered me a potential client. I even felt tempted by the idea. After all, it would be an easy way of getting a head start on the others, losing my virginity behind their backs. I didn't know how much it would cost, though, or how to go about it. As I thought about this, walking along the docks, I felt myself changing direction, briefly resolute and then, three steps later, resigned to inaction. Zigzagging like that, I must have looked drunk. In the end, I told myself, it was better not to do it that way. It was cheating. It wouldn't even have counted as far as Vincent was concerned. I gave the prostitutes an apologetic, almost guilty look, the kind of look I gave people when they asked me for a cigarette and I didn't have any. Head down, hands stuffed in my pockets, I walked home.

I lived twenty minutes from the centre of town, in a large suburban housing estate, with my parents and my brother Sylvain, who was two years younger than me. As I got home, I was surprised to find a light on in the living room. I looked at the clock: it had only just turned one in the morning. I felt as if I had been at the club for much longer.

My father was sitting on the sofa, peacefully watching an action film on the television, his feet propped up on the coffee table, his hands resting on his belly. He looked so serene, far from the madding crowds of the nightclub. Hearing me come in, he looked up and smiled. Every time, I thought I could see in that smile the brief hope that I would bring someone home with me, before the hope was dashed and his disappointment discreetly swallowed.

'Hi there. Did you have a good night?'

'It was okay.'

'Where did you go?'

'The Beach – that nightclub out on the docks.'

'Whoa, you went clubbing! I thought you didn't like that kind of thing. So, did you dance?'

'A bit.'

'Cool. It's still early though – didn't you want to stay out a little longer?'

'Nah, I'm tired.'

I went upstairs to the bathroom. My clothes smelled of cigarette smoke, sweat and alcohol. I put them in the washing machine. While I was brushing my teeth, I heard my mother in the hallway. She would often get up when I came home, ostensibly to use the toilet but really to check that I was okay, that nothing bad had happened to me. I opened the door to reassure her. She was in her pyjamas, looking very sleepy; as far from the tumult of The Beach as my father had been.

'Did you have fun?'

'Yeah.'

I kissed her on the cheek, then went to my bedroom. It was quiet and cool in there. I had the impression that my room had been waiting for me. I had an ambivalent relationship with my bedroom. I loved it as a sort of shelter from the world. But I hated it too, as the vessel of my solitude.

Despite my tiredness, I found it hard to fall asleep. My heart was speeding, as if the nightclub had followed me into bed. I saw it again in flashes: the lights, the mass of bodies. My penis grew hard, for no particular reason. I was surprised and annoyed by this. Why was it waking up now, like some old guy who'd fallen asleep and who only opened his eyes at the end of the night, after everyone else had left? I didn't want an erection now. It wasn't even a pleasant feeling. It was like a morning hard-on, cold and random. To get rid of it, and in the hope that it would send me to sleep, I started to masturbate. I tried to empty my head of thoughts, but The Beach remained there, indelible. Its image lingered, despite my best efforts to forget it, and the muffled echo of the music pulsed in time with my wrist.

DYLAN

2002

After taking my baccalaureate exam, I spent two years study-ing for a sales diploma at the local college, mainly because I couldn't think of anything else I wanted to do. My friends had gone off to an expensive business school in Nantes, the nearest big city to where we lived. I hadn't heard from Vincent at all, and I'd come to realise that I never would. All that remained of that friendship were a few oppressive memories, and that phrase *on the pull*, which haunted me like an unfinished task.

For two years I tried – in corridors, at bars, during parties at people's apartments. It wasn't just that I failed to pull. I failed on the most basic level of making friends. People simply slipped through my fingers. The distance between me and them was as vast as ever. They all seemed to have bonded with one another in my absence, as if I'd missed the icebreaker party at the start of term. But in fact I had been there, and I'd felt the same way even then. The problem lay with me. I found it difficult to have a conversation, for example. And that was pretty fundamental to making friends. To some people, it came naturally – they always found plenty of things to say, without even thinking – whereas I had a very small stock of phrases that I drew on to break awkward silences: How are you? Have you been here long? Do you think it's going to rain? That was it. I could never manage to reply to their replies. I wasn't interesting, and I wasn't very interested either, since I never took the time to listen to anyone. I was too busy thinking, trying to find things to say. Not even things, really, just phrases, words, sounds. It must have been embarrassing. People preferred to avoid me. Whenever they were forced to speak to me, I could sense them getting restless as soon as another conversation started close by, as if they feared missing some vital piece of information because of me. Although these difficulties occurred frequently, they weren't bad enough to suggest that I had some sort of handicap or an alibi of that kind. It was quite simply my personality. It probably wouldn't have taken much to change it: a new face, a different body or voice, a bit of humour or culture, a new way of bursting into rooms.

In 2002, I started weight-training.

I was twenty-one. It was the last summer before the end of college. In September I would have to start looking for an internship. My parents were on holiday (my father worked at the mayor's office, my mother at a medical laboratory), and Sylvain had gone with them. They were camping in the Landes, and I thought I was too old to tag along. I was bored on my own, though. I didn't have any real hobbies: I watched a bit of TV, played a bit of PlayStation, read a few comic books, but that was all. I had found a job at a bakery chain called La Mie Câline. Every morning, on the way to work, I would pass by Bodymax, the local gym. I kept shooting it furtive glances, drawn towards it by the idea that it might help me. One day, I went inside.

The interior was just as I had imagined: full of machines and metallic noises. It was like being in an ironworks. Loudspeakers pumped out techno music. Behind the reception desk stood a short but very muscular man, his arms and shoulders swollen and bulging with veins. His hair was spiked up with gel. He had a young face. As I got closer, I realised he was about my age.

'Can I help you, sir?'

'Yeah. I wanted to, um, join.'

'Please follow me to the meeting area.'

We sat on gym balls beside a coffee table. He took out some papers then smiled at me as though noticing me for the first time.

'My name is Dylan, and I'm the trainer here. I'm pleased to meet you.'

He was calling me *vous*, and he sounded weirdly robotic and respectful. I felt like telling him that he could talk to me normally, that we were the same age, that we might have been friends.

'So let's start with the basics. What is your goal?'

I blushed. I hadn't seen this question coming, hadn't even thought about how I would answer it.

'I don't know.'

I did know.

'Are you looking to bulk up a little?'

'Yeah, yeah, you could say that.'

'And for what reason? To make yourself more attractive?'

'No, no, not at all!' I said hastily.

'Hey, we don't judge anyone, here at Bodymax.'

'No, but really, that's not why. It's just because I want to ... stay fit, you know.'

His eyes quickly scanned my body. I tensed my muscles. I was wearing a skintight T-shirt, and I hoped he might mistake my jutting ribs for a six-pack.

'Could I ask you to step onto the scale?'

'I don't weigh much,' I warned him.

I stood on the scale and waited for the verdict.

'Eight stones nine pounds,' Dylan said quietly, his voice discreet and professional, like a doctor diagnosing a serious illness.

'That's really light, right?'

'Yes, it is.'

He screwed his face up in thought.

'I would recommend you sign up for our premium membership. It's a one-year commitment. Comes with a student discount and one hundred percent access to our gym equipment. Are you busy this afternoon?'

When they got back from their holiday, my parents and my brother were surprised. I had never liked sport, but now suddenly they discovered that I had become obsessed with lifting weights. My father asked me if I was sure about this. He suggested that swimming or cycling might be more suitable if I wanted to improve my fitness. 'Weightlifters tend to end up with ugly bodies.' I felt like telling him that his body was ugly. He was thin, with a round belly. The worst kind of body. Sometimes I hated him for giving me his genes, as if it was all his fault, and the fault of his father before him. But I remained polite. I said I'd given it a lot of thought, that this would help with my self-confidence. That was the right thing to say. He even bought me an Adidas tracksuit.

Weightlifting is an unusual sport. The first weeks were tough. I would go to the gym with my little bag, my little towel, my little body that was fully clothed and yet felt completely naked in front of all those bodybuilders who only needed a fleeting glimpse of one of my biceps to know the truth about me. I was a weakling. As such, I had to smile and nod when muscular men advised me about nutrition and anatomy. I pretended not to notice the condescending looks of guys who lifted much heavier weights than me. Sometimes I would spot other weaklings there and feel less alone. If I looked really hard, I was even able to find a few who were weaker than me. And then I could look down my nose at them. This is what's known as the food chain. At the top are the beefcakes, who go to the gym six times a week and grunt while they're lifting. They are stuck in an endless loop of bulking up and shredding. They are never satisfied. But therein lies the problem. Perfection does not exist. Muscular mass shrinks as quickly as it grows. It is a never-ending race to stand still. The gym is a giant air compressor: people go there to inflate their muscles, then rush outside to show them off – on beaches, in photos, at parties and in beds – before it's too late, before they get injured or old or dead. Weightlifters have various motives, each linked to a different complex. Mine was simple. I wanted to leave behind my skinny little body, and the life that I had carved in its image.

I was in my fifth week, and already looking more defined, when I heard Dylan mutter: 'Whoa, nice arse . . .'

I was on the rowing machine and he was standing near me, staring at a woman doing squats across the aisle.

I froze. Had he said it to me or to himself? Unsure, I half-smiled at him, then started rowing again. He edged closer, smiling mischievously.

'Did you see that, Arthur?'

Now I was stuck. He was talking to me like a friend. No more *vous*-ing, no more robotic respect.

'See what?'

'The arse on that girl doing squats over there.'

I shook my head and continued my exercises.

'Well, go on – check it out!'

Feeling pressured into it, I glanced up then lowered my head again, ashamed.

'So?'

'I saw.'

'Have you ever seen such a perfect peach?'

I felt a faint stirring of anger. I had been taken hostage and I didn't know how to escape. Whatever I said would just lead to even more embarrassing questions. I decided to shrug. But that wasn't clear enough. To make him shut up, I'd have had to say that I didn't want to have this conversation. As it was, he simply assumed I was questioning his taste in arses.

'Seriously? Man, you've got high standards! Well, I'll wait for you to show me a better one, okay?'

He smiled at me and held out his hand. I obediently high-fived him and he walked away. Naively I thought that might be the end of the matter, but the seed had been sown. In the days that followed, Dylan openly ogled other women's arses in front of me. He was obsessed. His entire working day was based around a series of bottoms. He was cunning: he never stared as they passed, but anticipated their arrival and waited for them to enter his field of vision, thus absolving him of all blame. He always had something to say about each one, and it was always to me that he said it. I blushed every time. It wasn't his vulgarity that offended me, so much as what was expressed through it – his lust, which reminded me inexorably of my own. Because the truth was that I wasn't coming to the gym only to get more muscular; I was getting more muscular to be more attractive, to give myself the courage to ask someone out. But I kept putting it off.

One Friday, as he was tidying up the gym, Dylan came over to see me while I was doing pull-ups.

'Man, I've seen so many cute arses today! I need to smash one, to get it out of my system. You want to come out with me tonight? You can be my wingman.'

'Where?'

'The Beach. You know it?'

I shivered. I had almost forgotten The Beach. The sounds, the lights, the smells, the massed bodies: all of this rose up inside me in a surge of acid reflux. I wanted to say no. But this was an invitation. An opportunity to make a friend. To finally take the plunge.

'Sure.'

The building was bigger than before. A giant cube. As I moved towards it alongside Dylan, I held my breath, trying not to think about it, not to remember. You had to pay to get in now. Five euros. We went inside. I walked up to the bar, taking care not to look at the dancefloor. Dylan followed me. He rested his massive arms on the counter-top. It was strange seeing him away from the context of Bodymax, like bumping into a teacher at the supermarket. I lit a cigarette. The barman shouted over the music: 'What'll it be?' For a second I panicked, then made my decision:

'Whisky and coke please!'

'What's that?' Dylan asked.

'Whisky and coke – it's good!'

'Not for me. I'll have an apple juice please.'

'You don't drink alcohol?' I asked, trying to sound offended.

'Never! There's nothing worse for your abs. Cheers!'

I clinked my glass against his. I felt strangely fine, or at least not too bad. Much better than last time, anyway, presumably due to the absence of Vincent. I liked the way that the club offered a total break with the outside world. The lighting was warm and subdued, and the volume was so loud that it freed me from having to talk. I also realised that a crowd of five hundred people was less oppressive than a group of ten. The tension of parties in people's homes, the violence of sofas, the unbearable discussions on balconies ... The horror of all this was taken down a notch, diluted by the sheer size of the room. I felt as if, here, I could start again, reinvent myself as someone stronger, more serene, shed my bland dullness like an old skin.

Dylan downed his drink and leaned towards me.

'Let's do this!'

Without waiting for me, he got up and went off to dance. Smiling, my inhibitions lowered by the whisky, I spun my bar stool in the direction of the dancefloor ... And then it was as if I walked into a glass door.

Beyoncé – 'Crazy in Love'

Out on the floor, nothing had changed. It was as brutal as ever. All I could see were men – heavy, muscular men in skin-tight, glossy black or white T-shirts – saturating the space, swaggering and barging like a herd of wildebeest. Now I noticed the women too, but above all the way the men were looking at the women. Their gazes were so strong, so insistent that they became a sort of substance, a thick manure spread across the nightclub, suffocating everything. Covering the ground, filling the air, poisoning the music. The idea of walking into that seemed impossible.

Dylan had melted into the crowd. He was one of them. He was dancing slowly near the palm tree, facing the mirror wall. His legs remained straight; only his chest moved in time with the music, pivoting from side to side. Elbows raised like a boxer, his arms followed the movement of his chest. With his eyes half-closed and his mouth half-open, he looked simultaneously tired and concentrated. To my surprise, he did not go near anyone else, even went out of his way to avoid contact with other bodies, as if he was afraid of messing up his muscles. He looked like a model, content to watch his arms in the mirror, as if his own presence was enough to make him come. He was a new person, all his lust evaporated. Maybe he was afraid to go on the pull. A reassuring thought. I was not the only one. It even crossed my mind that maybe he was a virgin too. Not that I would ever have dared ask him: it was not the kind of thing men our age could talk about. My virginity was written all over my face; it seeped from every pore in my body. There were people who remained virgins their whole life. I remembered Monsieur Sureau, a technology teacher at my old school, who lugged around that reputation on his back like a bagful of stones. Everyone knew that he was single and always had been. Sometimes we would laugh at him and sometimes we would pity him – it depended on the day – but, however kind he was, however skilled as a teacher, it was invariably his status as a virgin that people thought about whenever they saw him or discussed him, speaking in low voices as if they were at his funeral. Nothing else about him could possibly compensate for that unforgivable deficiency. I didn't want to end up like that. I still had the lukewarm dregs of my strength and pride, enough to help me avoid Monsieur Sureau's fate.

Without thinking, I dived into the mass of bodies, heart fluttering, and walked towards Dylan. He held out his hand and I high-fived him, maybe a little too enthusiastically. At first I stood motionless beside him, as if protected by his enormity. I watched him dance. All I had to do was imitate him. How difficult could it be? Hundreds of people were doing the same thing. I didn't know any of them, and I would never see them again, so it should be easy enough to ignore them. My body rigid, my eyes lowered, I began tapping my foot. Mimicking Dylan's movements, I swayed my hips, my shoulders. Deep inside my pockets, my fists unclenched. The tension of the music increased, the rhythm doubling, quadrupling, the beats growing so fast that they blurred together . . . There was a moment of silence, then the sound grew even louder than before, the bass notes vibrating the floor beneath our feet, and Dylan and the whole of The Beach started to jump up and down. Caught in the moment, I put my hands in the air and jumped along with all the others. I was doing it!

This time, the sensation was pleasant, maybe the most pleasant sensation I had ever felt. True, I was only jumping. True, I wasn't really dancing. But all the same, I felt like I was in sync with the others, in tune with them. The distance between us shrank. There was no longer a gulf, a void to be filled, and there was no need for words, friendship, humour or intelligence. All I had to do to be part of the crowd was to jump, swelling its ranks with my solitude, like a branch thrown onto a fire.

After a while, I met someone's eye: a woman who looked like she was on her own, in a T-shirt and jeans, wearing glasses and a kind expression. I forced myself to smile at her and she smiled back. No doubt about it: I'd made eye contact. Something was possible between the two of us: a dance, a kiss, maybe even a relationship. I took a deep breath and bounced sideways towards her. We found ourselves face to face, jumping in rhythm, my hands close enough to hers that I could reach out and hold them. But just as I was summoning the courage to do that, a man came spinning loose from the mass of bodies and danced between us, like a big fly, his back turned to me in a way that struck me as impolite. Wanting to believe that he had not done it deliberately, I moved delicately around him.

'Oi!' he yelled at me. I stared at him, terrified. 'What the fuck are you playing at?'

I retreated, waving my hands and still jumping a little bit. He must have thought I was making fun of him because he came after me, his mouth open and his arms outstretched. He was expecting an apology. He was tall and wiry. Silver bracelet. V-neck T-shirt, with tight-fitting sleeves that showed off his muscular biceps. I was about to run away when Dylan appeared out of nowhere, huge and reassuring.

'Hey, leave my mate alone!'

'Mind your own fucking business!'

The two of them fronted up, forehead to forehead, hands gripping each other's T-shirts, ready to rip them apart. Dylan must have weighed twice as much as his opponent, but V-Neck didn't back down. I stood watching them. I wasn't bouncing anymore. I'd lost my momentum, and my dance partner had disappeared.

'Come on, then! Come on!'

They grappled. A third man intervened, ostensibly to separate them, although I got the impression that he wanted to fight too. I watched over his shoulder as V-Neck threw a punch at Dylan. Soon some other men got involved and it became hard to follow what was happening. I found it shocking that the music didn't stop. Amidst the flying fists, I caught a glimpse of Dylan lying on the floor, his body looking much smaller as he curled up self-protectively. Two bouncers arrived. One of them grabbed V-Neck and marched him away, while the other helped Dylan to his feet. He was bleeding, his eyes were closed, and he was drooling a little bit. The bouncer, supporting him, led him towards the exit. I followed helplessly in their wake through the parted crowd. People kept dancing as they watched us, like car passengers when there's a wreck on the motorway. They looked outraged and happy. I could understand their reaction. The blows received by others can make you feel good, like blows that you have parried yourself. I was mostly thinking about the girl who'd danced with me. I couldn't find her anywhere. I would probably never see her again.

Outside, the wind was cold. V-Neck was pacing around the car park. One of his friends was trying to calm him down, but it appeared to be having the opposite effect. The bouncer sat the still shaky Dylan on the pavement.

'Don't ever try that again here, mate.'

And he went back to his post at the club entrance, without offering any further assistance. Stunned that he would just be abandoned like that, I sat down next to Dylan.

'Are you okay? Should I call for an ambulance?'

He buried his head in his hands. His enormous body was shaking. The goosebumps on his skin made him look even more muscular. He looked like a child bodybuilder. I didn't know what to do.

'Thanks for defending me.'

He didn't say anything. A group of women our age walked past us.

'They look nice,' I said shyly, trying to cheer him up.

He didn't reply. I watched them go past us and into the club. For a moment, I felt like leaving Dylan on the pavement and going back inside with them to jump around to the music.

Suddenly, he stood up and rushed at V-Neck. Panic-stricken, I ran behind him, but it was already too late. Besides, what could I do? They were already fighting. Dylan fell to the ground again. People yelled. Someone kicked him hard in the face and he stopped moving.

After his stay in the hospital, Dylan was on sick leave for quite a long time. To be honest, it seemed more like humiliation leave. His injuries healed fairly quickly, but the real injury – the memory of his shame – remained. He had been beaten up. His muscles had done him no good at all. His body, designed to dominate, had been laid low twice in a row by a weaker body. Six gym sessions a week had not been enough. It was a failure, an insult to his work and his masculinity. He might never get over it, I thought. At the very least, it would take time. And time was running out. Bodybuilding was an addiction. It even had a name. Dylan had told me about it once. Bigorexia nervosa. A few weeks without weightlifting was enough to make the bodybuilder feel withered, to become depressed, and finally to give up altogether – to get fat or skinny, depending on the individual. It must be a horrible feeling. I didn't see Dylan for a month.

In the end I asked the owner of Bodymax about him. He said Dylan had quit his job. I don't know what came over me then, but I told him I'd just finished college and I was looking for work. I certainly wasn't qualified to be a trainer, but if he needed someone to work on the reception desk, I was up for it. The owner said he'd let me know.

Dylan's disappearance motivated me to increase the amount of training I was doing. I went from working out three times a week to five times a week. To my parents' concern, I changed my diet: turkey and rice, tuna and rice, eggs, lentils, oatmeal, bananas, protein shakes. My life became devoted to weight-lifting. Nothing mattered to me anymore but my body and the desire to keep developing it. Bumps grew and veins bulged under my skin. Slowly, patiently, I transformed myself.

One night, I decided to go back to The Beach, alone this time.

We were having a family dinner with Sylvain's new girl-friend, Audrey. She was sitting opposite me, as polite as my brother, witty when she needed to be. My parents laughed at everything she said, but I didn't even dare look at her. Like a shy little brother, which is exactly what I'd become. I was born before Sylvain, I spoke before he did, and walked before he did, but he passed me suddenly when it came to girls. And when it came to everything else, for that matter: school, friends, hobbies. I dragged my feet in every aspect of my life. Especially in the most important aspect. When you're twenty-one and you still haven't kissed a girl, it's hard to concentrate on anything else, unless you're prepared to resign yourself to it forever. After dinner, alone in my bedroom, I listened to Sylvain and Audrey trying not to make too much noise in theirs, and decided to take action. Shower, shirt, aftershave. I went downstairs. My parents were watching TV. For the first time, they seemed perturbed to see me go out.

'Where are you going?' my mother asked.

'Out. Clubbing.'

'On a Tuesday night?'

I hadn't even thought about that.

'Um, sure. Why not?'

'No problem,' said my father. 'It's good to go out and enjoy yourself. Even on a Tuesday.'

'Who are you going with?'

I thought about telling them the truth.

'With some new friends.'

'Oh, that's good.'

Looking suddenly embarrassed, my father added: 'And if you want to bring someone home . . . you should, um, feel free, you know. This is your home, after all.'

My cheeks burning, I nodded then went outside.

In the street I felt slightly ashamed. I had never gone out alone before. Not even to the cinema. My parents would prob-ably have felt sad, seeing me walk on my own like that to The Beach. Oh well . . . too bad. I had an overwhelming urge to do it anyway. I wanted to dance.

FRANCK

2006

I went to The Beach every Friday and Saturday night. During the week, I worked at Bodymax and waited for the weekend. After my first payday, I had moved out of my parents' house and rented a tiny studio flat close to the town centre. Living on my own was a relief: I could no longer feel the weight of my parents' gaze on my solitude. I went to visit them every Sunday, feeling hungover. They asked me about my nights out. I said it would take too long to describe them. The truth was that I still hadn't managed to find anyone there. I knew what the problem was: I needed to learn to dance better. Dancing was the language of a nightclub, like swimming was the language of a pool. Bodies danced to express their desire, to awaken the desire of others, to bring those desires together. And I stammered.

One night in September 2006, I went to my first beginners' dance class at a gloomy recreation centre near the train station. I'd found it by googling 'learn how to dance in a nightclub'.

I had found courses for rock, salsa, Zumba, modern jazz, hip-hop, classical, and even Breton folk music, but there was nothing for dancing to the techno and pop music that they played at The Beach. Finally, I saw an ad that said: 'Club for amateur dancers. Learn to overcome your inhibitions and let yourself go. Dare to dance!'

Ten of us showed up to the class. All the others were older than me, most of them in their thirties. The teacher was a cheerful man who asked us to take turns introducing ourselves. I went second, which gave me time to prepare something in my head while the first one was speaking.

'Good evening. My name is Arthur. I'm twenty-five. I work at a gymnasium, where I look after clients and deal with paperwork. I also work out there, between noon and two every afternoon when the gym is empty.'

'No surprise there,' said the teacher. 'You have the body of an athlete. Do you have any other passions in life?'

'Yes. I go clubbing every weekend.'

Suddenly everyone looked more attentive.

'So you dance regularly?'

'Yes, and I like it. But I do have a problem.'

'Tell us what's on your mind.'

'I sometimes feel like I'm going round in circles.'

'That's very interesting. Could you be more specific?'

'At the nightclub I always dance in the same way, with the same movements. I feel a bit limited. I'd really like to be able to ... spread my wings, if you know what I mean?'

'That's very, very interesting. But there's something I'm curious about: when you're alone at home, do you sometimes dance? When you get out of the shower and you're listening to music, for example?'

'Yes,' I admitted.

'You have nothing to be embarrassed about. In those moments, do you feel more free than when you're dancing at the club?'

'Yes.'

He scratched his beard and narrowed his eyes at me.

'Arthur, would you say that you lack self-confidence?'

I thought about this. Maybe I seemed pathetic, sitting there so stiffly, my hands joined in my lap, as if I was about to issue a directive, and yet with such a lost look in my eyes. But I didn't know how else to sit. It was the fault of my arms, which were now so swollen with muscle that I couldn't let them dangle by my sides. I had to keep them slightly raised all the time. My self-confidence, what there was of it, was lodged somewhere between my right arm and my left arm. Unfortunately, I had not been able to develop that part of me the way I had the rest. In fact, every time it was exercised or put under pressure, it just seemed to atrophy even more.

'Yes,' I replied.

He nodded his head understandingly.

'That's what I thought. Arthur, where you're concerned, considering your situation and your experience as a dancer, I would give you only one piece of advice: you need to relax.'

That phrase made me tense up. I had heard it too many times before. The people who said it to me often had the same inflection in their voice: 'Just relax!' they would say, the last syllable sounding exaggeratedly bright and high-pitched, as though they were trying to cheer up a sulky child.

'You're right,' I said. 'Thank you.'

The others introduced themselves, one by one, each person announcing their name, their age, their occupation, and their problems with dancing. The one I remembered was Laura, twenty-seven, who worked in a bank and had absolutely no sense of rhythm. She was calm and pleasant, tall and heavy-boned, with lots of make-up on her face, and lips that were tight with embarrassment. Our eyes met for an instant and I looked away. The next time I shyly glanced up at her, she was no longer facing me.

'Good evening, my name is Franck,' the last man said. 'I'm in my thirties, I'm a botanist, and I would like to open up my chakras.'

'That's very specific, Franck. Very interesting.'

'Thank you. I know a few of the basics, but not much.'

'Well, we're here to work on them together.'

'Maybe I could show you?'

'Sure,' said the teacher, looking slightly taken aback.

And so Franck began to sway and undulate, his eyes half-closed, in a vaguely Tai Chi-like manner. The others watched him, looking very serious. Suddenly he stopped, relaxed his body, and smiled as if expecting a round of applause.

'Thank you, Franck. Very interesting.'

He bowed his head modestly. A tall, thin, pale man, dressed in linen trousers and a white shirt, his long hair in a ponytail, Franck corresponded to the idea that I had in my head of a washed-out old hippie. I thought his body was poorly proportioned. After so long spent working on my body, I had become very demanding when it came to other people's bodies. Too skinny, I would think. Too flat, too flabby. Sometimes I would feel a faint disgust towards people who didn't work out, who didn't strive to improve their appearance. In my opinion, physical self-discipline did not receive the respect it deserved. It was certainly less prestigious than professional success or artistic achievement, for example. If that hadn't been the case, I would have enjoyed a much higher standing in society.

The teacher put on some lively music and the session began. We had to wander around the room, all of us making the same basic little arm movements. The idea was for us to get to know one another by dancing in the same way. After that, each of us had to try different movements, to let ourselves go. Franck let go after about three seconds. He began windmilling his arms. He was a good dancer. Why was he taking a beginners' class? A rush of courage spread through the others when they saw him. The dam of their shyness burst, setting loose a powerful flood of ideas. One man started hopping about on one leg. A woman froze then began making tiny movements with her fingertips. The teacher looked pleased. Everything seemed to interest him. The slightest spasm was a victory. If someone had rolled around on the floor screaming, he would probably have encouraged them. I just danced the way I did at The Beach, looking around and picking up the best ideas for new moves, imagining myself trying them out on the dancefloor. In a corner of the room, Laura was struggling. Her movements were slow and clumsy. Now and then she would miss a beat like someone tripping on the stairs. I felt moved, watching her. I made eye contact with her and we exchanged what seemed to me a nice, friendly smile.

At the end of the session, I decided to go and talk to her. We were in the same class, after all, I thought, so what could be more natural? When I came out of the changing room, she was there, smoking a cigarette, her back turned to me. I took a deep breath and headed towards her, but she was already chatting with Franck.

'Arthur!' he called. 'I just wanted to say that I really liked your introduction. It was perfect.'

'Oh ... thanks.'

'It even made me want to go clubbing again.'

Laura seemed to agree with this by nodding her head slightly, which encouraged me to hang around.

'I've been chatting with Laura, who's lovely. I was telling her how much I liked the way she danced. Very restrained, you know?'

'Yeah ... Me too,' I muttered, blushing.

'You were good too,' she told Franck.

'Oh no, I was really bad ... But I'm here to learn. The teacher's cool, isn't he?'

We nodded. To get them on my side, I attempted a small criticism.

'Although he's ... I don't know ... a bit much, don't you think? I mean ...'

'Oh, you think so? I really like him. He allows us to work on our weaknesses, and to meet new people ... I think it's great that he's so invested in it.'

Laura shrugged. 'I don't know. I'll wait and see how the next session goes.'

It was then that Franck, with a spontaneity that was perhaps not entirely sincere, exclaimed: 'I just had a mad idea. Maybe the three of us should get together this weekend, so we don't have to wait for the next session? Arthur, you could take us clubbing on Saturday! It's the best way to train, right? What do you say?'

That I'd rather die than go there with you, I thought. Franck struck me as one of those people who are excellent at first impressions but whose charm is illusory, and who turn out a little later to be deeply irritating and unlikeable, doomed to wander endlessly from one new group of friends to another, like a bee gathering pollen. I had met people like that before, in the margins of familiar places: the common rooms at school and college; the water cooler in the office where I had worked as an intern; and the reception desk at Bodymax, where the loneliest clients would come and talk to me. I had to keep away from people like that, I knew. I was too impressionable, too easily influenced, capable of putting up with complete arseholes since I had no real friends of my own.

'Sure, why not,' said Laura.

'Sure,' I repeated.

On Saturday, after my weightlifting session, I stayed at home and watched dance music videos on MTV while I waited for the night. Late that afternoon, I cleaned up the apartment a bit. This was a ritual that I followed every time I was about to go out, just in case I didn't come home alone. I made my bed.

I vacuumed the floor. Every time, this gave me the ominous feeling that I was preparing my own sadness, that all these little actions would turn against me when I came home, reminding me of my dashed hopes. Invariably I would return alone, and the next morning, when a beam of sunlight illuminated the linoleum, I would think how clean my flat looked, like a hotel room, empty and impersonal, ready to welcome the next guest, and I would feel a stab of discouragement. Because nobody had ever come to stay at my apartment, so what was the point in keeping it so neat and tidy? But I continued all the same, just like people who never go out continue to get dressed every day, not allowing themselves to hang around the house in pyjamas, because they care about their dignity, because they feel bound to keep fighting against their loneliness, until something happens.

At ten o'clock I took a shower. I liked to do it at the last moment so I would feel fresh for as long as possible. I opened a can of beer. With the curtains drawn and a towel tied around my waist, I played 'Everybody' by Martin Solveig and danced on my rug. I was swinging my hips and rolling my shoulders quite well, but my legs still looked a bit stiff. It was my lower half that kept me rooted to the ground, stuck in the boring world of nights without music. Soon I would manage to tear myself free. Maybe even tonight, dancing with Laura. I put on my Zara V-neck, a pair of Calvin Klein boxer shorts, my black jeans, my Reeboks, my G-Star jacket that really accentuated my shoulders, and I looked in the mirror. Not bad at all. For a brief moment I almost felt fond of my solitude, because I was sure I would be rid of it in a few minutes. I never felt as optimistic as I did when walking to The Beach, with the day ending and my life finally on the cusp of a new beginning.

I got there early and lit a cigarette in the car park. I watched people arrive, on the lookout for a familiar face so that Franck and Laura might find me mid-conversation. Sometimes I bumped into people from my college there. They always arrived in a group of friends, already laughing and excited, probably because they'd been drinking in a bar or at some-one's apartment before coming to the club. There weren't many clubbers who went straight there from home, like I did, without stopping off somewhere for an aperitif. Especially not on their own. To make myself look less suspicious, I had got into the habit of gazing out into the distance as if I was waiting for some friends.

Laura arrived first. She was wearing a dress and even more make-up than before. Seeing her walk, I couldn't help think-ing how clumsy she looked. A vague sadness gripped me as I imagined her at home getting ready to go out, just like I'd done. Even so, my heart started to pound. That shared smile at the dance class had marked me; the sense that she might be even remotely interested in me had been enough to intensify my feelings for her.

We kissed cheeks. Neither of us made a kissing sound for the first cheek, but we both exaggerated the sound for the second one.

'Looks like a nice place,' she said.

'Yeah, very nice.'

I tried to think of something to say. I wasn't used to having

conversations here. Coming on my own made that unneces-
sary. Laura beat me to it:

'So ... do you come here often?'

'Yeah.'

Ask her a question, I reminded myself. You always have to
ask someone a question in return, like hitting the ball back
when you're playing ping-pong.

'You?'

'This is my first time.'

'Okay.'

There was a silence.

'Franck's late,' I said.

'Yeah. That's so Franck, don't you think?'

'Totally, yeah.'

Our eyes scanned the car park, in search of him. If we could
just see him arriving, even a hundred yards away, we would
be saved.

'Maybe he forgot ...'

Laura shrugged, and the silence went on so long that I
knew we couldn't break it ourselves. We held our breath for
what felt like a good minute.

'There he is!' I said at last, relieved – almost overjoyed – to
see Franck at the other end of the car park.

He was wearing the same linen trousers as before, with an
ugly Quechua fleece jacket.

'Do I know you?' he asked as he stopped in front of us.

Laura laughed, and so did I. He kissed her on the cheeks,
his arm reaching quickly around to hug her. With me, he
just shook my hand, as if we were about to play a game of

something. Or, to be more precise, as if I had just lost the game and he was telling me I'd played well.

I knew the bouncer at the entrance by sight, but he didn't seem to recognise me. There were a few of them, and they worked different nights. I smiled at him to help him remember me, but he just nodded in response. We paid and went inside.

I led the other two through the corridor, trying to look casual and relaxed. I would happily have gone in blindfolded to impress them even more. As I approached the door to the dancefloor, Franck suddenly overtook me so he could open the door for Laura. I'd seen him act the same way, with exaggerated chivalry, in the changing rooms at the recreation centre. He was the kind of man who opened every door he possibly could for women, even seeming to go out of his way to find more doors to open. He stood aside and refused to be thanked for the gesture, raising his hand to signify that what he was doing was normal – natural, even. What could Laura do? I thought I saw her hesitate when confronted with the absurdity of this manoeuvre, but she went through. Franck was so kind. How could anyone suspect him of anything at all? What right did I have to assume that all this thoughtfulness must hide a very different Franck?

The dancefloor was packed. It's often like that in September, when – bathed in the afterglow of summer – it's still warm enough to go out without a coat. Hundreds of bodies were crammed into the club, undetectable from outside. The dancefloor was a field we had come to plough, a hunting ground, a lake filled with fish, a market without rules, without pity. It is rare that anyone spends five hours macerating in their own sweat purely for the pleasure of dancing. People came here to find someone to take home. That was the whole point of a club like this. All the rest was myths and legends, the insolent plenitude of a few satisfied hearts.

Black Eyed Peas – 'Pump It'

Franck didn't so much dance as glide, as if he was moving through lubricated air. Everything about him was oily. His smile was happy, harmless, self-sufficient. All the same, I could see – between his bowed legs, under the linen – the heavy, swinging bulge of his penis. Everyone could see it, and I couldn't believe that he was unaware of that fact. No, he knew all right. The disparity between that shamelessness and his zen persona, I thought as I watched him, betrayed what he truly was: fake zen, fake cool, fake gentleman, the kind of guru who doesn't practice what he preaches. A depraved lecher. Exactly the sort of Dark Franck I'd suspected him of being. Laura showed no wariness as she danced facing him. She laughed to fill the silence. Inch by inch, Franck edged closer to her, so subtly that he appeared to be moving without meaning to, pushed forward by the wind or the slope of the floor. Looking into her eyes, he began windmilling his arms again. She laughed even louder. I wanted to step in, to stop this happening. I couldn't bear the idea that they would end up together. Their bodies were only an inch or two apart when the music abruptly changed. Franck looked surprised. He wasn't a clubber, so he probably expected the song to fade out slowly, the way it would on the radio. The suddenness of it broke the spell between them.

They stopped dancing for a second, and I took advantage of their stillness to say:

'Shall we get another drink?'

Laura nodded. They followed me to the bar. I ordered three whisky and cokes.

'This round's on me!'

I put my money on the countertop. My nights out were costing me a fortune. The prices had gone up. Six euros for a drink. Eight euros to get in. On average, I spent about twenty-five euros a night. I wasn't rich. All my spare cash went on bodybuilding, clothes and The Beach. I economised on everything else: bought all my food at Leader Price, managed without a car and very little furniture, never went on holiday and had no other hobbies.

We sat on the terrace, a recently constructed veranda over-looking the club's rear courtyard. It was bathed in a subdued, yellowish light that made people's bodies look calm, warm, beautiful. I stayed on the margins of the conversation. A two-person dialogue was complicated enough for me; with three, it was even worse. I was constantly getting lost, blurting out phrases and grunts of agreement at random. So I listened as Franck talked about what a great place this was, and how all of us were making progress, and how nice of me it had been to bring them here. He wanted it to become a ritual for the three of us. He was only on his second drink, but I could tell he was already quite drunk, presumably because he wasn't used to alcohol. His face was turning red and he was smiling beatifically. He didn't seem to realise that this transformation was occurring.

After a while, Laura stood up.

'I'm going to the bathroom.'

'I'll keep your place!' Franck said.

As soon as we were alone, his expression grew more serious.

'Are you okay, Arthur?'

'I'm fine.'

'I wanted to ask you something ... Man to man, so to speak.'

I looked at him questioningly. He knocked back his drink, then took a deep breath.

'What do you think of Laura?'

'Laura?'

'Yeah, Laura.'

He looked quite tense suddenly.

'I think she's nice. Very kind.'

'Yeah, that's for sure. But what I mean is: are you ... how can I put this? ... Are you interested in her?'

'What do you mean?'

'You know what I mean.'

Feeling accused and guilty, I decided to lie.

'I'm interested in her ... as a person, of course.'

'No, I mean, are you after her?'

'After her?'

'Do you want to pull her?' he said finally, his voice growing more high-pitched with irritation.

I didn't know what to say. He stared at me seriously. So, he considered me a rival? I felt almost flattered.

'Listen, Arthur, I've got nothing against you ... We're

talking man to man, right? I just get the feeling that there's something between Laura and me. This is really important to me, you see. I'm not just in it for a quick fuck, okay?'

I was shocked by his sudden vulgarity.

'But ... neither am I. I don't understand why you would say that.'

'I'm not the kind of guy who thinks with his dick,' he went on, eyes wide.

'Neither am I! Stop it!'

All of a sudden, I felt hot. I didn't want to raise my voice. Whenever I got angry, it was always me who got hurt. Franck was about to reply, but Laura reappeared on the terrace. He leaned towards me.

'Mum's the word, all right?'

He fell silent then, but remained in the same position, as if letting his words echo inside my head. I realised that he had bad breath. The rancid stench of creamy petit fours. The lingering odour of his hidden putrefaction. I wanted to stand up to him. After all, I was much more muscular than he was. I could scare him, even beat him up if it came to it. But that thought made me feel ashamed, and I changed my mind.

'All right.'

We went back to the dancefloor. Franck danced discreetly to the first few tracks. I avoided his gaze, avoided making any sudden movements. The atmosphere was unpleasant. I felt sick. All around us, I could see other men who looked just like him, with their aggressive lust, their competitive faces, as if nothing excited them more than the thought of crushing their rivals. I thought about leaving. But then, insidiously, Franck started moving closer to Laura again, his mouth half-open. I don't know what got into me then … Maybe it was the alcohol, or a surge of pride or desire … In any case, a kamikaze determination drove me to start dancing better, moving my legs, trying out every routine that came to mind, imposing my body on the dancefloor, and finally, quite naturally, holding out my hands to Laura. Surprised, she grabbed hold of them. We danced together. Our movements meshed, our bodies came closer. I looked over at Franck: he was still nearby, mouth hanging open, frozen in the same dance loop, like a scratched record. Our eyes met. For an instant I thought he was going to attack me, but something completely different happened: his face twisted into a disturbing expression of mingled jubilation and amazement, and he raised his hand like he wanted to congratulate me with a high five, as if we were best friends and he had always believed in me or something.

'*Yes!*' he shouted in English.

We looked at him blankly.

'*Yes yes yes!*'

He pointed at us like we were champions. Then he started to circle us, clapping his hands so hard it must have hurt. It wasn't just the alcohol; he was losing it.

'Stay there, you two!' he yelled. 'I'll be back!'

He danced his way towards the bar. Laura stared at me wide-eyed, and we burst out laughing at the same time. I felt like I was floating then. Our bodies moved even closer, until they were glued together. We were on the verge of kissing.

'*YES! YES! YES!*'

Franck returned with three fluorescent shots, carried in a

triangle above his head. He looked like a madman. Laura and I laughed again; his behaviour was creating a complicity between us. Laura rested her head in the hollow of my neck. Franck gave a long high-pitched wail then, a sort of wildly joyous ululation. For a second I thought he was about to collapse. He handed us the shots, then downed his own, his head thrown back, his ponytail spinning. He threw the empty glass to the floor. People flashed him looks of outrage. Laura freed herself from me.

'Franck, are you okay?'

She was still laughing a little, out of politeness.

'Oh yeah! *YES!*'

He started clapping again. Someone shoved him. He was swept away by a tide of bodies, disappearing into the crowd.

'What should we do?' Laura asked.

'Maybe we should leave him to it.'

She hesitated, then: 'Do you want to go now?'

'Sure! Do you want to come to my place?' I replied without thinking.

'Sure, why not!'

Not giving myself time to chicken out, I grabbed her hand again and started to drag her towards the exit. She looked around for Franck.

'Should we tell him goodbye . . . or not?'

'Nah, we'll see him at the dance class.'

I never saw him again. In my mind, Franck remained eternally in the limbo of The Beach, searching for new friends, new prey, dancing and laughing and howling, with tears in his drunken eyes.

*

Laura and I didn't talk much on the way back. We barely even looked at each other. I felt like the slightest movement would be enough to break the improbable equilibrium that was carrying us back to my apartment. We crossed the bridge, walked along the Loire docks, passed three roundabouts and went through the side streets of the deserted town centre. I had been this way so many times before, but it looked different to me now. I felt as if my life was about to change forever, to finally get started. Apart from my parents (when I first moved there) and a plumber and a guy from the gas company, nobody had ever come to my apartment before.

As I went in, I turned on the ceiling light and realised for the first time how stark and unpleasant its white light was, like the lights in the bathroom at The Beach. Everything was shown too clearly. I thought about turning it off and putting on my bedside lamp, but that seemed too steep a plunge into intimacy.

'It's very tidy,' said Laura.

'Thanks.'

We took off our jackets and sat at my table. I got up again to pour us two beers, but once the sound of the foam had faded to silence in our glasses, there was nothing but the two of us. No shadows, no crowd, no music. Laura took the initiative. She started a conversation about the evening, then about our jobs, then about some other things that I wasn't really listening to, because I was too busy looking at her, wondering how I could kiss her. I didn't know. Although I did assume that we both wanted it, given that we were there together. I drank my beer quickly, hoping that the alcohol would dissolve my fears,

or hers, that one of us would make the first step. All I had to
do was lean across the table or walk around it. It would have
been so much easier if we'd been sitting side by side. Here
again, it was Laura who managed to find a solution. She went
to the bathroom and, when she came back, sat quite naturally
on the edge of my bed. I hesitated for a moment then, surfing
the first wave of courage, went over to join her. Now we were
sitting very close, without any other obstacles, on my neatly
tucked-in duvet. My knees were shaking. I forced them together, while continuing to drink, automatically, from my
empty glass. I don't know how much time passed after that.
It was as if we were waiting for some external event to occur,
like two people sitting at a bus stop. Finally a moment came – I
sensed it – when Laura turned to me, so I turned to her too
and we looked at each other. Slowly our gazes descended to
our mouths, and our faces leaned in for a kiss. I didn't know
how to do it properly. I kept my lips shut. Laura delicately
opened them with hers. The taste of saliva disturbed me. She
put her hand on my shoulder, my chest, my abs, stroking my
muscles, which – under her touch – seemed to melt one by
one, leaving only my original body, skinny and nervous. Her
hand moved down to my jeans. I would happily have stopped
there for the night – that seemed like plenty to be going on
with – but instead I let her do it.

'Can we turn off the light?' I asked.

'Okay.'

I got up. The light switch was only a few steps away. I
walked slowly. Darkness fell. I wished I had shutters so I
could make the room even darker. When I turned around, I

saw that Laura had taken off her clothes. She sat waiting for me in her underwear.

'Get undressed,' she breathed.

Standing in front of the bed, I obeyed. I stripped off quickly and without thinking about what I was doing, as if I was getting ready for bed. First I took off my T-shirt, then my jeans and socks, balancing on one foot at a time. Now I was wearing nothing but my boxers.

'Those too . . .'

The last time I'd been naked in front of someone, I had been fourteen, in the changing rooms at the table tennis club where my parents had enrolled me, forced to take a shower with ten other boys, all of them laughing, used to being naked in front of one another. It seemed to me that nothing separated those two exposures, as if the ten years had not passed and I was still a child. We lay on our sides and she rubbed herself against my erection. The sensation was moist and pleasant. I couldn't believe this was happening.

'Do you have any condoms?'

I had one in my wallet – I'd kept it there for a long time – as well as a box hidden in my bathroom cupboard, but they must both have been past their sell-by date. It wasn't this that held me back, so much as the idea that Laura might think I had planned all this, buying the condoms because I expected to get her in bed.

'I don't think so,' I said.

'Hang on, I must have one in my handbag.'

She stood up. I didn't dare watch her walk. I still preferred the abstraction of our embrace, that submersion of our bodies

in absolute closeness. She helped me put the condom on, then
sat on top of me. It felt the way I'd imagined: hot and envelop-
ing. I didn't manage to really enjoy it, though. I was outside
of the moment, outside of myself. I came quickly. To make up
for this, I tried to help her come. I stretched out beside her and
caressed her with my fingers. I didn't dare use my mouth. My
fingers moved faster and faster. I could smell my own skin
more than hers. My arm was burning. I didn't know where
Laura was anymore; it felt like she was miles away. I got the
feeling that she was ready to be done with it too. We kept
trying for a bit longer, then she put her hand on top of mine
to tell me she'd had enough.

I nuzzled against her. Only then did I feel the happiness
spread through me. This was all I wanted: to hold someone
in my arms. The silence lengthened, the darkness thickened.
I was no longer in my bedroom, I was drifting slowly away,
our bodies so entwined that I couldn't tell where hers began
and mine ended. I was falling asleep ...

Then she whispered:

'I think I'm going to go home.'

Those words hurt my feelings. I'd been hoping to wake up
with her the next morning.

'Are you sure? I don't mind if you sleep here.'

'Thanks, but I'll sleep better in my own bed.'

'Okay.'

She stood up and got dressed in silence. I did too, just so I
wouldn't have to lie there. She picked up her jacket and her
handbag, turned on the light and carefully scanned the room,
as if the last thing she wanted to do was forget something, as

if the last thing she wanted to do was ever come back here, ever see me again.

'Well … good night, then.'

'Thanks. You too.'

She kissed me on the cheeks and left. The sound of her footsteps faded in the stairwell. In the stark light, all that remained were my unmade bed, the empty beer cans on the table, the hum of the fridge. I thought about The Beach then, and quickly went to bed so I could go back there as soon as possible.

WASSIM

2008

That Friday, I got there just after ten to enjoy the calm before the David Guetta concert. The Beach wasn't full yet. You could still see the floor. The atmosphere was cool. I sat at the bar, facing Alicia, the barmaid. She had joined the club the previous year. She wore a vest, with a sweater tied around her waist, and soberly mixed cocktail after cocktail, offering brief snippets of conversation and keeping the men who hit on her at a safe distance. I had never even thought of Alicia in that way. Not that I didn't like her – she was kind, honest, and elegant in the way she mixed drinks – but the simple fact was that she stood on the other side of the counter, off the dance-floor, off the menu, and that distance between us had made room for a precious relationship that could be described as a friendship, even if it was confined to The Beach. She was my only female friend. Relationships without strings were fairly compartmentalised here, and I found it easier to interact with men. Not that I did that very much either. In fact, Alicia was my only friend, full stop.

'I don't know how they managed to get David Guetta to play here ... I mean, he's a cut above the DJs they usually invite. Maybe he knows the owner, or he's got some sort of emotional attachment to the town ... Anyway, it's great publicity for the club. There'll be a lot of hot girls out there tonight, so get ready ...'

She gave me a free whisky and coke, then went off to help her partner, who I never talked to. Spinning around on my bar stool, I looked at the women on the dancefloor.

I dreamed of having a girlfriend, someone with whom I could hold hands, go to the cinema, go for walks, and make love in the middle of the afternoon. I had never found anyone like that here. From time to time, thanks to the improvements in my dancing, I had managed to kiss a girl and to end up at her place or mine, but the relationship always ended there; they never spent the night with me. Afterwards, I would hope for some sign of a future together, even if it was just eating breakfast at the same table, or swapping phone numbers, or a goodbye kiss of the kind that couples share when they're going their separate ways for the day – *see you soon* ... But none of this happened. None of them ever wanted a relationship with me. It was all over by the next morning, when I found myself alone, in my studio flat (which was sometimes annoyingly untidy, as though it wasn't mine anymore), or in an unknown neighbourhood, from where I would commute to work, hungover, without getting anything to eat, brooding guiltily: Was I bad at sex, bad at conversation, just not the kind of person that anyone wanted to see again? Probably. Conditions were never in my favour. It was often late at night, she was drunk and in a rush to get it over with. I needed more time, more gentleness. Maybe I was simply looking for love in the wrong place? It was possible that most of the people who went clubbing were in search of nothing more than that, a one-night stand, repeatable only in the case of certain criteria that I did not meet. There were other ways to meet people. Dating apps, bars, the street, holidays. But with all of these methods, I always came up against the same problem: how could I initiate contact without dancing? How could I ignite the first spark anywhere other than the dancefloor? All the other places nearby seemed somehow closed off to me, uninviting. No, I was only capable of going up to someone, looking in her eyes and holding out my hands to her when I was at The Beach. So I kept going back, three times a week now, from Thursday to Saturday, plus public holidays, without ever giving up hope.

Around ten o'clock we were joined by a friend of Alicia's: Wassim was about my age (twenty-eight), a tall man with a swimmer's body and a nice face. He was wearing a navy blue shirt tucked into a pair of canvas trousers of the same colour, with the belt showing. His Stan Smith sneakers were the only casual thing about him. He looked like he had come straight from the office, leaving his briefcase in the cloakroom and smiling to offset the seriousness of his appearance. After we'd introduced ourselves, he ordered a mojito and said he wanted to go for a smoke. Alicia was busy serving drinks, so I had to go with him to the smoking area. I was afraid we would have nothing to say to each other, but he made conversation quite naturally as he lit his cigarette.

'So have you been here before?'

'Yeah, I come several times a week.'

'Oh wow, so you're a real clubber! And you never go any-where else? To bars, I mean, or parties?'

'No, I don't really like that stuff.'

'I get it. There's probably not much going on around here. This town looks kind of dead to me. So you never want to try other clubs in other cities?'

'I'm fine here.'

I had tried once. I'd caught a bus to Pili-Pili, a nightclub in the countryside, about ten miles from where I lived. Everything there had struck me as strange: the architecture, the dimensions of the dancefloor, the music, the best spots for chilling or pulling, the shapes of the glasses, the taste of the whisky. I felt as lost as I had on my first night at The Beach, back to square one. It had been a terrible night.

'So I guess everyone must know you here?'

I started to wave this away with a gesture of humility, but I was feeling pretentious so I changed my gesture halfway through and put my hand through my hair instead.

'I know quite a few people here, yeah.'

This wasn't true. I knew Alicia and the bouncers, and that was it. The other faces were always changing. The town wasn't *that* small.

'Don't tell me you know David Guetta!'

'No, I don't know him.'

'I was kidding. Anyway, it's cool that you're so faithful to the same club. I think that's a beautiful thing.'

He smiled. I liked the way he was trying to get to know me through The Beach, instead of asking me 'what I did in life'. That was often the first question. I didn't like answering it. I didn't feel like my job defined me. I felt profoundly bored whenever that kind of subject came up at the club, like when I was a child and the adults at the dinner table started talking politics.

'What about you?' I asked. 'Do you come here often?'

'No, this is my first time. I live in Paris. I do go out there, but not to this kind of place. I'm here tonight to see Guetta. I love his stuff, don't you?'

'Yeah ... He's a cut above,' I said tentatively.

In reality, I didn't have an opinion about David Guetta. For me, all the music they played at The Beach sounded the same. The melodies and the words hardly mattered. All that counted was the beat. I could dance to David Guetta, Lady Gaga, Pitbull, Magique System, Akon, Justin Timberlake or anyone else as long as there was a regular beat. All other kinds of music were a total turn-off. I'd tried listening to Mozart and Pink Floyd and everything else that the internet came up with when I typed – in English – 'best music of the world'. None of it had any effect on me, no matter how long I spent listening to it. Anything without a beat was just vapour to me.

Wassim changed the position he was standing in. He seemed to think for a moment, then put a hand in his pocket.

'I've got some E if you're interested?'

'Some what?'

'Ecstasy.'

'Oh, right, Ecstasy. I didn't hear you properly the first time.'

I blushed. I had never taken drugs. They scared me. Sometimes I would see dealers hanging around the car park, or even in the club's bathroom.

'So, are you interested?'

'Sure, why not?'

'We can take a tab now if you like. That way, it'll kick in before the concert starts.'

'Good idea.'

He opened a small plastic sachet and discreetly shook out two coloured tablets. I tried to look relaxed, but inside I was panicking. What was I supposed to do? I remembered the first cigarettes that Vincent gave me at school before I'd learned how to smoke. This kept happening: people kept giving me things to inhale, swallow or absorb, and I had to figure out what to do with them while they watched, on the lookout for a mistake, as if there was some honour in consuming drugs or alcohol, as if drug-taking were some manly pursuit, a skill to be honed, a form of courage. Thankfully, Wassim seemed more kindly. He swallowed his tablet with a mouthful of mojito, and all I had to do was copy him.

'Thanks.'

'My pleasure.'

We went back into the club. The music had improved and people were arriving. The place was coming to life. A smile escaped me. The equilibrium didn't consist of that many

elements: the style of lighting, the density of the air, the tex-
ture of the floor ... In any case, I felt at home here. It was the
ideal setting, sealed off from the outside world. I rushed onto
the dancefloor and started dancing lightly, catching the eyes
of a few girls, feeling that unmistakeable excitement rise up
within me: the night had begun.

For now, I felt like hanging out with Wassim. Spotting
an official photographer in the distance, I suggested to him
that we should get our picture taken together. He laughed,
surprised, and followed me over there. Photographers came
here sometimes, wandering around with their cameras. I
liked to subtly make my way into their field of vision, so
that they would take shots of me without me having to ask.
Occasionally, when I'd had a few drinks, I would work up the
nerve to pose with a group of strangers. You had to be quite
supple to insert yourself into the frame like that, whether
to one side or at the bottom of the image. I always struck
the same pose: thumbs up, muscles tensed, my expression
serious but with raised eyebrows, as if surprised to find
myself there. If the person next to me wasn't openly hostile,
I would interact with them, pointing them out or putting a
hand on their shoulder. That way, I managed to appear in
one photograph after another, like the character in *Where's
Wally?*, multiplying my presence. The next day, the photos
were published on an official website, 'Soon Night', touched
up so that everyone looked beautiful and shiny. I would
find all the ones in which I appeared and post them to my
Facebook timeline, adding a comment beneath each one:
'What a night!'; 'Fun times on the dancefloor'; 'Maximum

coolness', etc. I didn't get many likes, because I didn't have many friends. Ninety-three, to be precise. They were mostly people I'd known at school or college, a few Bodymax clients, and several family members. My aunt, whom I barely knew, would sometimes leave comments under my photographs: 'You look like you're having a great time. Yours, Christiane.' I discreetly deleted them all.

'Say cheese!'

Wassim struck the pose naturally: thumb raised, relaxed smile. I felt proud to be photographed with him. At least it seemed credible that we might actually be friends. That was rarely the case at The Beach. Most people did not appear interested. They already had plenty of friends. They came here looking for something else. I understood, of course, but was that really a reason to neglect friendship? At the bar, in the smoking area, on the terrace, conversations would spring up easily enough, but they never lasted more than a few minutes. The press of bodies kept people mingling, and anyone who vanished into the crowd rarely reappeared, like drowned swimmers. Here, thirty feet was the equivalent of infinity. But at least the problem contained its own consolation: there were always new people to meet.

We went back to the bar to have another drink and wait for the concert to start. Wassim talked about himself a bit more. He was the head of marketing at Franprix, a supermarket brand that didn't exist in this region. He liked music and sport. He lived alone. He really seemed like a nice guy. I couldn't wait to see him dance: only then would I truly get to know him. An hour on the dancefloor was worth more than

all the CVs, ID cards, discussions and lists of hobbies in the
world.

At midnight, David Guetta entered the DJ booth. Everyone
started screaming. As always on a big night, there was a fierce,
electric joyfulness in the air, something almost vengeful, as
if we were all throwing the accumulated frustrations of the
week onto the floor before trampling them underfoot. It was
then that I started to feel the effects of the drug. My body
felt hot and I panicked, worrying that I was about to lose all
control. And then, suddenly, my mood stabilised. The temper-
ature cooled. Distances shortened. I was effervescent. I felt a
wave of love for the whole world.

David Guetta – 'Love is Gone'

Wassim was a really good dancer. I couldn't discern any
repetition or routine in what he was doing. Lots of people here
were content to string together a few familiar movements.
They were easy to spot. I had my own tics: elbows in and fists
raised like a boxer; palms opening one after the other to mark
the off-beat; thumbs wedged in my belt during transitions
between songs. Wassim seemed to evolve continuously, like
a long melody. He improvised. And more surprisingly still,
he smiled. Not many people smiled while they were dancing. It was too serious for that. Most of them wore a look of
sullen concentration, the same kind of look people have when
they're masturbating or praying. But Wassim, in the middle
of the dancefloor, was smiling as if he was happy. He shone.
Eyes were drawn to him. Women sought out his presence. He
joined in their game without attempting to hit on any of them,
grabbing hands, moving from one body to the next, creating

a communal movement. He really looked like he was there to dance rather than on the pull. I had never seen that before. Feeling blissful, I tried to imitate him, letting the music guide my movements. It was amazingly easy. Wassim made me better through his simple presence. The sound flowed. David Guetta's blond locks waved above his turntables. The lights, the colours, the rhythm and the other bodies all became part of me. I even forgot why I had come here in the first place.

My happiness climaxed when he played 'Love is Gone', my favourite song. 'Are you hot tonight?' Guetta asked, his voice echoing as if we were in a stadium. And spontaneously, without any embarrassment, I joined in the general roar of assent while bass notes rose up from the centre of the Earth, shaking the floor, vibrating our guts. I looked at Wassim, whose mouth was closed. His head was thrown back: he was staring at the ceiling. Nobody here ever looked at the ceiling – I didn't even know what it looked like – so I threw my head back too, and saw a tangle of cables, gutters and spotlights. Then Wassim dragged me by the arm, and I realised that he had spotted an air vent. Right underneath it, we continued dancing in a cool breeze blown down from above. Suddenly I understood exactly why I loved this so much. I had known it for a long time without ever being able to put it into words: in dance, life fell into place, settling into a system of rhythms and movements where even the silences followed a certain logic; it was as if a giant grid, a familiar filter, had been superimposed over what had always struck me as chaotic and uncontrollable.

When the song ended, Wassim put his mouth close to my

ear and told me that he wanted to go for another smoke. We pushed our way through the crowd, away from the dancefloor. It was hot in the smoking area too. Wreaths of smoke choked the light. The music pulsed, muffled, through the door.

Wassim smoked with his back to the wall.

'You're a really good dancer,' I said.

'Thanks. You're not bad yourself.'

'I've never seen anyone dance like that before.'

'Shall I tell you the secret? You have to think about cavemen.'

I looked at him, intrigued. He took a long drag, eyes closed, then went on:

'So, at the dawn of humanity, right, people used to dance together in divine rituals. That was the high point of dance. Everything else has been a fall from grace. Okay, long story short ... The Greeks arrive and decide that dancing is beautiful. It becomes an art form. Later, of course, kings get interested in it, like the sheep they are. They ask to see shows, and the ballet is invented to satisfy them. That was the end of transcendence. In the nineteenth century, Johann Strauss turns up – the greatest DJ in history. His thing is the waltz. Now, people stop dancing in groups and start to pair off. Everyone gets excited about this. It becomes a method of seduction. It all speeds up: tango, swing, rock, and then night-clubs are invented. Slow dances become fashionable. People think this is going to bring them closer, but in fact it's the op-posite: each couple is isolated in its own little bubble. There's nothing communal anymore. You might think we've reached the lowest point now, but there's worse to come: computers bring techno music, Jeff Mills and all that. This creates solo dancing. Each person stays in his own corner. So that's where we are now, more or less. If it continues like this, in thirty years' time there won't be any more nightclubs. People will just stay at home and dance with a screen. I don't want that. So we need to get back to the caveman days when people danced in circles, not to try to pull, not even to have fun, but simply to be together ... in a sort of divine moment. So, anyway, that's my theory, for what it's worth. What do you think?'

I drank in his words.

'I agree ... You seem to know a lot about this stuff.'

'I'm just interested in it. I don't know much apart from that.'

He lit another cigarette. I tried to think of something in-telligent to say.

'So, when you dance ... it's really just for the sake of dancing?'

'Yeah.'

'You're not trying to pull at all?'

That made him smile.

'Well, when it comes to that kind of thing, this club is not really the best place for me.'

'Why?'

'It's just not my thing.'

'What do you mean?'

He raised his eyebrows, as if I were missing something obvious. I wasn't sure I understood.

'I prefer boys.'

I was surprised, but I tried not to show it.

'Oh, yeah?'

'Yeah. And there aren't any here. Not my kind of boys.'

'What makes you say that?'

'Just look around.'

I did. This amused him.

'So, do you see any?'

'I don't know.'

He smiled at me. There was a disturbing intensity in his eyes as they gazed at me, as if he was, through that gaze, making my body exist, giving me substance and solidity. I sensed his desire, and the thought crossed my mind that I could kiss him. Maybe that was the solution to my problems, to all my impossible tomorrows. Maybe I had been mistaken from the beginning. Maybe I had, without realising it, been barking up the wrong tree all this time? I had to try, at least. I thought I was capable of doing it, here, now. We stared at each other.

'Are you sure?'

I didn't reply. He came close and kissed me softly.

No, that didn't have any particular effect. In fact, it seemed to diminish the evening's intensity, which was, I realised now, a result of the drug stretching itself over my loneliness. Wassim must have noticed this, because he let go of me.

'Sorry,' I said.

'I'm not surprised. I didn't really think it was your kind of thing.'

'I thought I wanted to, but ... now I don't think I do. I'm a bit lost.'

'It's okay. I like the fact that you're honest about it. There's not enough honesty in the world. If you don't want to, you shouldn't do it. I do the same thing sometimes, forcing myself because I'm in a nightclub. I think that's what makes me sad. I should stop. Deep down, the only thing I want is to be in love.'

I was moved by his words.

'Yeah, me too.'

Out of nowhere, a surge of emotion rushed from my heart into my throat. I smiled to stop myself crying. Wassim saw this. He put his hand on my shoulder.

'You're having trouble with that?'

'A bit, yeah.'

'Don't worry, you'll find it. You're good-looking, a good dancer. It's just because you're different. You need someone who's different too. It's hard to spot people like that in a crowd. But they are there. Every night, there are some of them. You need a bit of luck and a bit of time, but you'll find them.'

He looked at his phone.

'I should get going. The E is starting to wear off, and I don't want to take another one. It was a good night. I'm glad I met you. Take care of yourself.'

We said goodbye like friends, but I had a feeling I would never see him again. I didn't even know his surname. Wassim. He left.

Three in the morning. I hadn't noticed the time passing. People were looking at me. In the bright light of the smoking area, their bodies suddenly seemed too present, too heavy, too anchored to the ground. I was weak and I felt cold. To regain some stability, I went back to the dancefloor. It was packed. Everyone was jumping up and down to 'Baby When the Light'. I melted into the mass of bodies, forcing myself to dance like Wassim had danced: generously, fluidly, serenely. *You'll find them,* he'd said. Around me whirled so many beautiful faces. The nightclub was like the drum of a giant washing machine. All I had to do was stay here. Let it carry me where it would.

SYLVAIN

2010

On the night of my thirtieth birthday, my parents threw a surprise party for me at their house, inviting my Aunt Christiane,
my brother Sylvain and his wife Audrey. The two of them
lived in Rennes now, where they had opened a bike rental
shop. They were expecting a baby. I was going to be the kid's
godfather. The idea struck me as weirdly abstract. It gave me
a sort of automatic pride, tinged with an ache of melancholy.

We had aperitifs and I opened my presents. In recent years,
nobody had known what to give me, so they would just put
cheques in coloured envelopes, but this time they'd all made
the effort to choose something for me: I got two simple, nicely
designed Colourful Standard T-shirts from Sylvain and
Audrey; a bottle of vintage champagne from my aunt, who
said I should save it for a special occasion; and a floor lamp
for my apartment from my parents. My mother insisted that
it was not a problem if I wanted to exchange it, but I said it
was fine, I liked it. Or, to be more accurate, I didn't dislike

it. The truth was I didn't really have strong opinions about objects like that. My mother would drop by my apartment once or twice a year, supposedly for a coffee, and each time she worried about the blankness of the décor there, fearing that it must be affecting my mood. Or, worse, that it was the reflection of some inner emptiness. But to me, my apartment was just a place where I slept, ate and waited to go out to The Beach. When I finally had a girlfriend, I thought, I would decorate it – or move somewhere else.

During the meal, I knew, two subjects of conversation were likely to be brought up, probably by my aunt: my body, and my nights out. The first came up when I was helping myself to more chicken. Christiane remarked that I had a big appetite, presumably because I needed the protein. Casually, she then asked if I was taking any supplements. I made the usual arguments: yeah, but they're all natural, just milk protein powder, nothing to do with steroids. All the same, she seemed to continue to doubt the authenticity of my body, as if I was cheating, as if I had stolen it. In her eyes, there was something suspicious about my transformation. She had known me long enough to have watched it happen, to remember the skinny me. In fact, that me was still visible in my slender, fragile face, a constant reminder of what I had wanted to stop being, suggesting that my big arms, my big pecs, my broad back and all my muscles were somehow fake. Even my parents could no longer hide their embarrassment about this. Especially my father. He listened to my aunt and I knew he didn't disagree with her. Over the years, the optimism he had felt at seeing me exercise and go out at night had shrunk to a kind of incomprehension and mute condemnation. His smile had frozen, like someone hearing a once-funny joke for the thousandth time. He worried that I was burying myself in clubbing and muscle. I avoided the subject. The inevitable consequence was that we spoke less and less.

Things soured over dessert. Christiane, her tongue loosened by the Muscadet, decided to ask me: 'So how's your love life, Arthur?'

I laughed nervously. My parents played dead. Audrey shot me a brief smile of sympathy. She had always been very kind to me. Maybe too kind, as if she felt sorry for me.

'Do you have a girlfriend?' my aunt insisted.

'Not really.'

I did have Marlène though. Our relationship may have been uncertain, but it should have been enough for me to be able to call her 'my girlfriend' in front of my family. I could have spent the rest of the meal telling them about Marlène if I'd dared. My parents would have been happy. This was all they were hoping for. They wanted evidence that my chosen lifestyle was leading somewhere; they wanted to be reassured, rewarded for all the years they had spent encouraging me to meet people, to have fun. One word would have been enough to soothe all their anxieties: Marlène. But I didn't pronounce it. The gulf between her and them was too vast. The idea of talking about her here seemed every bit as absurd as imagining my parents dancing at The Beach. They were two different worlds. As people liked to say when describing two opposing things, they were 'day and night'.

'I imagine you meet lots of girls, though.'

'Some,' I shrugged.

'Do you still go to your disco?'

'They call it a "nightclub" these days,' my mother whispered.

'A nightclub, of course. So what I'm wondering is: can you really meet someone you like at a nightclub?'

'Of course you can,' said Sylvain. 'That's the whole point of it.'

'But what I mean is: can you meet someone who ends up as your girlfriend, not just a brief flirtation?'

'You'd have to check the statistics,' my brother went on, 'but I think the answer is yes. Lots of couples meet in nightclubs.'

'And you, Arthur ... Would you be ready to meet the love of your life at your nightclub?'

I shrugged and felt myself blush.

'Yeah.'

There was a silence. I poured myself another glass of wine and stared into space, hoping this would make Christiane stop interrogating me. She observed me with her ethnographer's eyes.

Audrey tried to come to my rescue.

'I think it's a bit tyrannical, this obsession with everyone being part of a couple. It doesn't have to be that way. Lots of people are perfectly happy without it.'

'Ah, okay,' said Sylvain. 'Well, I guess I'd better get going then ...'

He motioned as if he was about to stand up, and everyone laughed. He quickly sat down again and stroked Audrey's arm. I watched them enviously. They did not hold hands or

put their arms around each other, and they rarely kissed in
front of us, but that very distance suggested the depth of their
love, the infinite time they had for embraces, the absence of
any urgency, the space left free for silence, simple pleasures
and occasional solitude. I wished that I, like them, could be
serene enough to think about other things, could sometimes
have moments when I didn't yearn for love.

Everyone went to bed before midnight. They had arranged
for me to spend the night there, even though I lived only a
twenty-minute walk away. I didn't like being in my childhood
bedroom. Every time, seeing my old desk and my poster of
New York, seeing my comic book collection and all these
things left where they had been before, as if I'd died, I felt overcome by a vague sadness. So I stayed in the kitchen and took
the bottle of Muscadet out of the fridge. It wasn't whisky, but
it was drinkable. I was a little bit drunk. The others thought
they were too – they laughed at having drunk too much and
worried about how they would feel the next morning – but
they weren't drunk: they had no idea what real drinking was,
what a real hangover was. I thought wistfully of The Beach.
I missed it. Stuck here, I felt miserably that I must be missing
a great night out, that something important was happening
there, without me, behind my back. Alicia had told me once
that this anxiety had a name: FOMO. Adolescents in particular had suffered from this fear of missing out since the rise
of social media.

The kitchen door creaked open. It was Sylvain.

'What are you doing here on your own?'

'I'm not tired.'

'Is everything okay?'

I nodded. Looking unconvinced, he sat down opposite me. He glanced at the wine.

'You drink a lot, don't you?'

'It's my birthday,' I said. 'It's normal.'

He flashed me a complicit smile and poured himself a glass, but I could tell that he didn't really want more wine. It was just a technique to win my trust.

'It was a good night.'

'Yeah.'

'Even if Christiane was a bit much ...'

Narrowing his eyes, he mimicked her:

'Now, Arthur, you'll have to take me to your disco one of these days!'

I smiled.

'You know,' Sylvain said, 'I get the feeling you haven't been very happy lately.'

Here we go, I thought. Our parents had probably sent him to check on me. He was their emissary. Here to say the things that they were too afraid to say.

'Sometimes I think it'd do you good to do something different with your life ... Travelling, maybe, seeing the world ... And, well, you know what Christiane was talking about? Being a couple and all that ... I mean, I know it was a bit over the top, but maybe she's right ... Maybe you'd be happy if you could settle down with someone, don't you think?'

Suddenly I made my decision: I would introduce him to Marlène. Otherwise this shit would never end. It was time to bite the bullet. I could introduce her to my brother this very night. She was bound to be at The Beach, as she was every Friday. Sylvain would give a sanitised version of events to my parents. And that would be a relief for everyone, me included.

'Do you feel like walking into town?'

'Sure. I'll just let Audrey know, and then we can go.'

It took a certain courage to go dancing in December. Lots of clubbers only come out in the summer months, like mosquitoes and tourists. I loved The Beach in every season. Each had its own particular charm. In winter, walking through the corridor and leaving my coat in the cloakroom reminded me of the hot chocolates of my childhood, rain on windows, long Sundays spent watching TV in pyjamas.

When we reached the docks, close to the bridge, Sylvain froze.

'Hang on ... Where are you taking me?'

'Clubbing.'

'Are you kidding?'

'No. Why?'

'But everyone's at home.'

'They're asleep.'

He looked at me like I was mad.

'You can't do this to me. It's seedy.'

'Come on, just for a while. Please. I'd really like to show it to you. And it is my birthday ...'

He looked thoughtful. He must have pitied me.

'I'm not dressed for it.'

'Neither am I, but that doesn't matter. It's not a special night.'

'All right. But just for half an hour, okay?'

When we crossed the bridge and I felt the familiar smooth- ness of the tarmac car park under my feet, I breathed a sigh of relief. We were on the right side of town. My whole body relaxed. I lit a cigarette.

'You smoke?'

'Only when I come here.'

I would have to quit someday. But it was difficult to manage without this little stick between my fingers that gave me an excuse not to talk, that justified my solitude when I went to the smoking area. Or any place where people couldn't dance.

As we got closer, Sylvain became my little brother again. He started making pointless gestures – taking out his phone and putting it back in his pocket, adjusting his shirt collar – and I felt the urge to reassure him.

'It's got a really great atmosphere, you'll see.'

'I've been here before. Back when I was still at school.'

'Oh, really? Great! How many times did you go?'

'Just once.'

We reached the entrance.

'Hi Alassane,' I said to the bouncer.

'Hi Arthur, how are you?'

'Fine, thanks.'

'That's good, that's good.'

He looked at my brother, who smiled back nervously.

'I'm guessing you two are related?'

'Pleased to meet you,' said Sylvain, holding out his hand.

Alassane shook it, amused.

'All right ... well, have a good night. Make yourselves at home.'

'Good night,' said Sylvain as he went inside.

He didn't notice that I had got him in for free. He probably didn't even think about it. Following me along the corridor, he made a show of not being surprised by anything, as if he knew the place so well, but this was a technique that I had used myself many times. I could see that he was ill at ease, that the bass pounding up from the floor was making him tense. This gave me a sort of strange pride. My life was here, behind that door, and I was ready to show it to him.

Rihanna – 'We Found Love'

'Go and sit down, I'll be back in five minutes.'

He walked along the wall until he found a table. I shoved my way through the crowd of drinkers to reach the bar. I asked Alicia if she'd seen Marlène and she said yeah, in the middle of the dancefloor. Already wasted, she added.

Marlène was there, dancing uninhibitedly. I stopped for a moment to observe her from a distance. She was tall and dynamic, her body sheathed in a summer dress. Alicia thought she was trashy but I found her beautiful: I liked her angular nose, her belligerent attitude, the way she danced as if she was angry. I would have liked to describe her better, to talk about the person she really was, but I knew almost nothing about her. Nothing except for her body, discovered in the darkness of The Beach or inside her parked car. I had met her here two months ago, on the dancefloor. We had danced with a single body from the very start, like a couple who'd been rehearsing. People had stopped to watch us. She had kissed me, caressed me, suggested we go outside, and taken me to her car. There, behind the tinted windows, with Fun Radio blasting out of the speakers, we had made love. She'd sat on me, gripping my whole body tightly, but I had not managed to make eye contact. She looked like she was fighting with her eyes closed. Her orgasm had made me come, and it had not been followed by any sadness or emptiness. I had clung to her afterwards, but she had gently freed herself and told me that she preferred to sleep alone. I had gone away obediently, without even asking for her phone number, stupidly, because I didn't want to bother her. In the days that followed I had hated myself. Then, the next Friday, miraculously, she had reappeared on the dancefloor and we had started all over again. We had settled into a rhythm now. No dates or tender words. We found each other by chance on certain nights, we went from the dancefloor to her car, and from sex to nothing at all. While we were together, I could tell that Marlène liked my body more than who I really was. She never looked at me, hardly ever kissed me. Even so, this was not just a casual fling, I felt sure of it. My feelings for her grew in silence. Soon I would confess them to her. I was in love.

'Hi Marlène!' I called, gliding in front of her.

She was dancing with a man who was crudely thrusting his pelvis at her, his hands held either side as if to keep her penned in. She cried out when she saw me and threw herself into my arms.

'Arthur! I was looking for you everywhere!'

Alicia was right: she did look drunk. Maybe high on cocaine

too. Sometimes she would offer me a line in the bathroom and I would refuse. Ever since the night of the David Guetta concert, I had steered well clear of drugs. I was afraid of catching an overly violent glimpse of happiness, or something of the kind. I preferred to stick to what was within reach.

'It's my birthday!' I told her, dancing casually.

'Seriously? Oh, we should celebrate! Come on, let's get a VIP box!'

I followed her.

'I'm here with my little brother. Can I introduce you?'

'Totally!'

'The thing is, I've never told him about you before,' I added anxiously. 'So maybe it'd be better if we said we were together. You know, just to simplify things?'

'Don't worry, I've got this!'

Leaning on the bar, she yelled at Alicia that it was my birthday and asked if we could have a VIP box. She gave it to us on the house, along with a bottle of champagne and a flaming shot instead of a candle. Carrying them at arm's length, we walked towards the classy, glow-in-the-dark banquettes located on a raised platform in the shade of the palm tree. Normally, it cost at least a hundred euros to sit here. You had a perfect view of the whole club, spread out at your feet.

I went to fetch Sylvain. He was still sitting in the same spot, legs crossed, looking at his phone.

'Come with me – I want to introduce you to somebody!'

Frowning, he followed me.

'This is Marlène, my . . .'

'His girlfriend!' she shrieked, opening her arms wide.

He looked at me uncomprehending for a second, then hastily smiled and held out his hand.

'Nice to meet you, Marlène.'

We sat down. She opened the champagne bottle and the cork went flying.

'Happy birthday, Arthur!'

Sylvain, looking completely disorientated, raised his glass to toast me. I felt nervous, but also proud and happy. Marlène's arm was wrapped around my waist and we looked like a real couple. We might have been sitting together like that at a restaurant, or even at my parents' dining table three hours earlier, and everyone would have imagined we were boyfriend and girlfriend. I thought about the vintage champagne that Christiane had given me. That was kind of her. I would have liked to drink it with Marlène in my apartment. After a short silence, Sylvain leaned towards her.

'So what do you do in life?'

'What?'

'You have to speak louder, Sylvain!'

Looking around nervously, he shouted: 'I said: what do you do for a job?'

I listened, curious. She had never talked about her work before.

'I work for a travel agency!'

'That's a high-growth sector!'

She nodded and giggled. He seemed to be waiting for her to ask him what kind of work he did, but she just poured us some more champagne and squeezed my thigh. I was starting to feel uneasy. Sylvian forced himself to keep smiling. His tensed face unwittingly reflected Marlène's expressions, like someone concentrating too hard as they watch a film.

'And how did the two of you meet, if that's not too indiscreet?'

She laughed again. I tried to signal to her.

'On holiday!' she exclaimed.

'Oh, really? Where were you?'

'In ... Croatia!'

Sylvain shot me a suspicious look. She had gone too far. I stood up abruptly.

'Let's go and dance!'

Marlène jumped to her feet. Sylvain stared at me as if I had broken a solemn pact.

'I'd rather not, Arthur. It's not my thing ...'

'Oh, come on!' yelled Marlène. 'You need to relax a bit! I bet you're just as good a dancer as your brother!'

'No, I really don't think so!'

But she tugged his arm and he was left with no choice. We stood together near the edge of the dancefloor. To repair some of the damage, I danced as well as I could with Marlène, so that at least my brother would know how well-matched our bodies were. I loved dancing with Marlène. Ever since my conversation with Wassim, I had preferred dancing with someone rather than on my own. It was an empathic art form: you had to respond to the movements facing you, to invent counter-rhythms, echoes, lightning-fast synchronisations. When I danced, I was transformed. I could see it in the looks of other people, and in my reflection in the mirror wall. I looked more handsome. I wished that the whole world could see me that way, that everybody I knew could be here.

Sylvain appeared awestruck, watching me. His own body was stiff as a plank, one foot tapping in time with the beat.

'COME ON, SYLVAIN!' Marlène screamed.

His nose creased by the forced smile he wore, Sylvian seemed determined to do the strict minimum of dancing. He would clap his hands randomly, out of time, and look around as if hoping to hail a taxi. Almost against his will, his gaze lingered on the bodies of the women around him, sliding downwards before frantically, guiltily staring into space. He looked like he was trying to stay afloat in a swimming pool. With his skinny legs and his knobbly knees encased in denim, he looked a little gauche. Men rarely paid enough attention to their legs. They were obsessed with their torsos and their arms, but the legs were usually neglected. I was irritated by the sight of long, thin, ugly legs like my brother's and my father's; they reminded me of what I used to be. Seeing Sylvain looking so lost here, I felt detached from him, as though he was on the other side of a window, and in the same instant I was overwhelmed with sadness. He didn't like The Beach, didn't like Marlène; he had nothing to say to her and would never see her again. For him, all of this was just a moment, a brief favour, a head poked through the half-open door of my nights.

When the song ended, he stepped towards me.

'I'm going back!'

'Already?'

'Yeah, it's late, and I don't want Audrey to worry. But

thanks for inviting me – it was fun! You're a hell of a dancer! And it was nice to meet your . . .'

Instead of finishing his sentence, he just gestured at Marlène. He gave her a quick wave, and she waved back while continuing to dance.

'Please don't come back too late to Mum and Dad's house. It'd be nice if you weren't hungover for brunch!'

He sidled away, taking care not to touch anyone as he passed, as if he was extricating himself from a row of seats at the theatre.

'He's not much fun, your brother!' Marlène said, grabbing hold of my hands.

I didn't reply. I just danced with her so I wouldn't have to think.

The music kept playing and time stretched out. After a while, I felt turned on, so I said:

'I want you.'

'Come with me . . .'

It was raining outside. People hurried across the car park, trying to keep their high heels, gelled hair and ironed shirts dry. The club was an island, its neon lights gleaming on the tarmac and on the waters of the Loire, while the rest of the town lay in darkness all around us. With our coats over our heads, we ran to Marlène's car. She put Fun Radio on at full blast and we stripped off. This time, while we were making love, the emotion became too much for me and the words came out of my mouth in a rush.

'I love you . . .'

'What did you say?'

'I ... Nothing.'

She stopped moving. She turned off the music.

'Arthur, I heard you. You shouldn't say stuff like that.'

'Why not?'

'I don't know ... It's a turn-off ... You can't love me – we barely know each other.'

She pulled herself away from me. Her body was stiff with tension. I could feel my chin quivering. It was a solemn moment and I wanted us both to react to it that way, but Marlène just seemed annoyed, violently banal. I didn't try to persuade her. I was afraid I would make her even colder towards me. Already my dreams had been reduced to the hope that she wouldn't think too badly of me when she re-membered me in the future.

'Sorry,' she said.

'No, I'm the one who's sorry. I don't know what got into me.'

'It's okay, let's just forget it. I'm tired now. I'm going to go home.'

'You shouldn't drive. You've had a lot to drink ... Let me call you a taxi.'

'I'll be fine.'

I dropped the subject. She always drove home in that state.

'Be careful. Good night, Marlène.'

She gave me a tender look, stroked my arm, then started getting dressed again. I got out of the car. Behind the tinted window, she seemed to disappear. Her car set off, crossed the bridge, went along the docks, and vanished.

I walked outside for a bit. Body tensed, I waited for the pain to come, the way I did whenever I stubbed my toe. There was a knot in my throat. My chest heaved. Everything I saw seemed sad and vain: the umbrellas racing across the car park, the customers under the awning, the empty town. This must be what heartbreak feels like, I thought. I didn't know where to go. The idea of returning to my parents' house chilled me: tiptoeing through the hallway, sleeping badly, waking late, secretly taking some Tylenol, going downstairs and finding my family all fresh-faced and happy in the garden, meeting Sylvain's eye, avoiding my father's, feeling my mother's gaze upon me, lying again, not being able to cry.

I took out my phone: it was one in the morning. It wasn't my birthday anymore. The club, though, would be open until six. I had almost the whole night ahead of me. I couldn't think of a better option, so I patted my hair, put a stick of gum in my mouth, and went back to dance.

ISABELLE

2014

Time was passing more quickly than before. I could sense this at every level: nights, weeks, months, seasons, years. I remembered the weekends of my childhood, the endless summer holidays. I was starting to get a feel for the actual duration of a lifetime, to sense its contours, to understand that everything would go faster than expected, and that consequently I needed to hurry up a bit if I didn't want to die alone. Other people were charging into adulthood; I could see it on Facebook. On my friends' timelines, photographs of drunken nights out had insidiously given way to images of smiling couples and their children, happy families in identical suburban homes, as if they had all gone to live in the same distant neighbourhood, without waiting for me. And all of this gave me the same gloomy feeling that I got when my nights at The Beach came to an end, when the music fell silent at 6am and the bouncers shepherded out the last few clubbers, each of us going back to our real lives like children returning to school after playtime, leaving me alone, my heart pounding, my body tight with frustration, the sun in my eyes. I was thirty-four.

In July 2014, The Beach was closed for three weeks for renovations. I walked past on the first day. There were trucks and tarpaulins. Apart from a few little details – the unlit neon letters, a few old flyers in the gutter – there was nothing left to suggest that this was even a nightclub. It could have been a gym or some old warehouse. Everyone had left, to who knows where, abandoning me in the car park, forgotten.

At Bodymax, too, I felt at a loss. There was no longer any reason to look at the clock, nothing left to wait for. The urgency of a meeting was diluted by the general slowness and the vacuity of days without nights, work without reward. Here, nobody came to talk to me. The clients no longer needed me since memberships had been digitalised and training screens installed. My only tasks were to stand behind the reception desk, put equipment away and water the plants.

There was a man of my age, a fairly fat guy who wore T-shirts with jokes on them, who paid for a premium membership and came every day to run on the treadmill without making any noticeable progress. Each time, he would place his phone on the tablet facing him and type into the same interface, which I thought I recognised. Alicia had told me about it before: it was a new dating app that a lot of people were starting to use. According to her, everyone would end up meeting each other on there. There would be no further need for physical interaction. I found this idea terrifying. This time, though, watching the client scroll through faces as he jogged on his treadmill, I decided to try it myself. Just during July. It was either that or three weeks of isolation.

And so, sitting behind the reception desk, I created a Tinder profile. First you had to choose some photographs of yourself. I selected three: an official portrait taken at The Beach; a topless shot taken in front of the bathroom mirror, and an older photo, taken one Christmas Eve by my mother, with the rest of my family cropped out. You could add a profile. I wrote: *Clubber in my spare time*. The profiles of women in the area started appearing on the screen of my phone, each showing their name, their age, and their distance from me: a few miles usually, sometimes even less. I had to swipe them left or right depending whether or not I liked them; if they liked me too, we could have a private conversation. It was soulless, disembodied. There were no looks, no movements, no smells. The inanimate faces all looked alike. I felt like I was leafing through a furniture catalogue without any real idea of the style I wanted. I got a few matches and struggled to make conversation with them. *Hi how are you?* My first attempts fell flat after a few messages. And then I received one from a certain Isabelle, thirty-seven, 1.2 miles away, no profile, with only one passport-style photograph taken against a white wall. Her face was beautiful, if a little stiff and severe, her hair tied in a ponytail. She wrote to me:

Hi, I like your photos.

I tried to think of a response that would not be too mundane.

> Thanks. I didn't know what to put.
> This is my first time on Tinder.

Welcome to purgatory. What are you looking for?

> I don't know ... meeting
> someone. What about you?

Same. Would you like to meet up in real
life? I don't like talking through text.

I accepted, blushing unseen behind the counter.

We arranged to meet that evening at the Rock'n Beer, a bar in the town centre. Showered, scented and nicely dressed, I arrived fifteen minutes early to get my bearings. I had not set foot in this kind of place since I was a teenager. The air here was heavy, static. Barely forty people in total, all of them seated, some on the terrace and some at the bar. Three men at the back of the room were playing a game of electronic darts that made more noise than the music coming through the speakers: rock music with no bass. I headed towards a table in a quiet corner, and as soon as I began walking I felt a strange disconnect, as when you set foot on an escalator only to find it's not working; in places full of noise and crowds, I was used to moving by dancing. When I was finally sitting down, I looked at the other people. They were talking, their cigarettes and their mobile phones placed on the tables in front of them, as serious as if it were the middle of the working day. It seemed difficult to establish any kind of contact. The groups were ready-formed, at independent tables, the shape of the evening decided in advance. Sitting there alone, I felt horribly conspicuous. To make clear that I was expecting someone, I kept looking at my watch with a preoccupied expression.

Little by little, my stress level increased. I felt as if I were waiting to take an oral exam. Which wasn't entirely untrue: after all, I would have to get to know someone through spoken words, sitting motionless while facing a stranger. Our messages had not suggested any particular shared interest, so we would have to find them by trial and error, constantly coming up with new topics of conversation. I tried to make a mental list of ideas, but that just stressed me out even more because I was afraid I would forget them, so in the end I just sat there and waited without thinking.

Isabelle arrived dead on time. She looked like her photograph: stiff, tall and skinny. She was wearing a plain jacket over a black shirt, a pair of tight-fitting jeans, and high heels. She scanned the room, as though in a hurry. I smiled at her and she came over. We greeted each other, leaned across the table to kiss cheeks. She sat down, took off her jacket, hung her handbag under the table, and placed her phone in front of her. Then, having nothing else to do, we looked at each other. She had bags under her eyes. To break the ice, she said mechanically:

'Have you been here before?'

'No, this is my first time. I usually go to The Beach, but it's closed.'

'The beach? Which beach?'

I didn't manage to conceal my surprise.

'Um ... I mean The Beach, the nightclub on the docks of the Loire.'

'Sorry, I don't know it. I never go clubbing. So you do?'

'Yeah, it was in my profile.'

'I'd forgotten that. So do you go there often?'

'Five times a week.'

Now it was her turn to be surprised.

'What? How do you manage with your work?'

'I can cope with hangovers. I'm used to them. Besides, my job is pretty easy. I work behind the reception desk at the gym. There's never anyone there in the early afternoon, so I can take a short nap without anyone noticing.'

Her face did not show many emotions; I found it hard to read. In that moment, it seemed suspended somewhere between embarrassment and curiosity. The waiter came over to take our orders.

'A whisky and coke, please.'

'And I'll have a coffee.'

'Espresso? Americano?'

'Espresso.'

I was afraid that she was already bored of me. Had she ordered a short drink so she could escape as soon as possible, feeling obliged to consume something first?

'Sorry, I know it's not very fun, but I need something to wake me up. I'm exhausted from work. I fall asleep at ten o'clock every night these days ...'

'Oh, yeah, that's early ... Ten o'clock is when I go out.'

She gave a little nervous laugh.

'What job do you do?' I asked quickly.

'I'm head of communications at a civil engineering company.'

'Sounds interesting . . .'

'No, not really. But it's a living, and I don't know what else I could do. The problem is it takes up all my time.'

'You never go out?'

'Apart from on Tinder dates, no.'

'You should give it a try, to chill out a bit . . . It might even make you more efficient at work,' I suggested.

'By going clubbing, for example?'

She was smiling now, but I still couldn't read her expression. I felt myself blush.

'Sorry, you must be bored of hearing me go on about that.'

'No, not at all! You seem really passionate about it. I like that – it makes a change. Tell me more. What do you like so much about that place?'

I thought about it. I had never put my feelings for The Beach into words before. She waited calmly.

'It's like, when I'm there, anything seems possible. The atmosphere is so different from the daytime. People are more open, less stressed. You can approach them. All you have to do is dance together . . .'

'And you never get tired of it? Don't all the nights blur into one after a while?'

I shook my head and tried to explain. I could have told her about the dull routine of my days, of my boredom at work and all the little repeated actions I had to carry out from morning until evening: getting up, getting dressed, grabbing my keys, leaving for work, going home again, going to bed, all of it done automatically, blindly, like someone moving through a dark room without banging into anything because they know the layout so well. But I changed my mind because I didn't want to sound depressing.

'I ... I would say that my nights are more varied than my days,' I said simply.

She smiled.

'That's quite persuasive. It even makes me want to try it out. The only problem is that I can't dance.'

'I could teach you,' I offered spontaneously, then immediately regretted coming on too strong and waved my hands in apology.

She laughed, more full-throatedly this time, more happily.

'You're funny.'

She watched me for a moment in silence. Her face had relaxed. Her eyes were brown and intelligent. I thought she was pretty. She blew on her coffee.

'Shall we get going?'

'Um, already?'

'Yeah, I don't really like this place.

'Okay ... Yeah, me neither, in fact.'

I hurriedly finished my whisky and coke. The coke tasted too sugary and the glass was too heavy, difficult to hold in my hand. Isabelle paid for both of us. That was fine with me: I still hadn't eaten into my week's wages. I took my wallet out anyway, just to be polite, but she said that I could pay her back in dance lessons.

Outside, she asked: 'What do you feel like doing?'

She spoke the words with the falsely casual tone that I had heard many times before, the one people use when they don't want to go home alone. I didn't want to either, but I felt suddenly afraid that she was only interested in sex, that she would sleep with me once then immediately dump me. On the other hand, the surprising ease of our conversation made me want to continue it outside of my usual haunts, to make the most of it, to do new things, the kind of old-fashioned date stuff that, in my mind, always boiled down to long walks through town, looking in the windows of shops.

'We could go and see a film,' I suggested.

She looked surprised again.

'Uh, sure ... I wasn't expecting that.'

'Or we could do something else, if you prefer.'

'No, I'm sorry, it's just me being stupid. That's a very good idea. I haven't been to the cinema for a long time – it'll make a nice change.'

She smiled at me and we walked to the Gaumont, a few streets away. I hadn't been there myself for a while. A long time, in fact. Years. My last memory of going to the cinema dated back to adolescence, when I used to go with Vincent and my friends from secondary school. What I remembered most clearly was our silent battle to sit at the centre of the group, the same as in the cafeteria; a battle that I always lost, finding myself shouldered to the end of the line, forced to twist my neck to participate in the conversation during the trailers. Since then, I had not felt any desire to return. And it had always struck me as absurd, almost humiliating, to go to the cinema on my own.

We decided to see *Gravity*, the George Clooney film about outer space. I really liked the décor of the room, all red and black, hushed and anonymous. We sat at the back. I found it hard to concentrate on the film. When I was still a teenager and I used to imagine myself with a girlfriend, my fantasies were always set here, in the cinema, my arm around her shoulder, a bag of popcorn between us, the light from the screen flickering over our faces. That image was as clear and precise as a real memory. And yet, that night, Isabelle's hand, placed on our armrest, seemed to me impossible to touch. An inch or two separated us, and it was a gulf. I knew she wanted it to happen too – I could sense it – but that small, simple gesture was impossible for me. I lacked the momentum. So I just kept my hand next to hers, where she could see it. At some point in the middle of the film, she took hold of my hand. I didn't move after that.

On the way out, Isabelle asked me if I wanted to go to her place, and as we walked there she asked me what I'd thought of the film. I didn't have an opinion, so I just said: 'Not bad.' But she hadn't liked it at all and she started to explain why, using very precise arguments that impressed and convinced me. I ended up agreeing with everything she said, changing my opinion completely, and this made her laugh.

'Yeah, you're really funny.'

'Sorry.'

'Stop apologising! Being funny is a good thing.'

She lived in a dull residential area in the south of the town. Her apartment was large but impersonal, decorated in an understated way. It was very clean, but not because it was cleaned on a regular basis, I thought; more because it never got dirty, because she didn't spend much time there. In fact, it was a lot like my apartment, only twice the size and way more chic. While she went to fetch us something to drink, I paced around the living room, examining it with discreet curiosity, since that seemed to be the done thing when you're invited to somebody's apartment at such an early hour.

'You can put some music on the computer if you like. I've got Spotify.'

'What kind of music do you like?'

'I never listen to music ... So put on anything you want.'

I pondered this. Several ideas came to mind, each one bringing with it a flood of memories. I went for a song by Chris Brown featuring Lil Wayne, 'Loyal', with a laid-back beat and a vocal track midway between rapping and singing, which seemed appropriate to me. When the first notes played, I watched for Isabelle's reaction. She smiled. She was opening a bottle of white wine on the kitchen countertop. I walked over to her. Without meaning to, I started dancing.

'Oh, wow, okay, you're really putting me on the spot ...'

I stopped.

'No, keep going. I like it.'

I started again, feeling intimidated at first, as though I was naked without the crowds of people and the spotlights and the throbbing bass. Then, looking at Isabelle, my inhibitions faded. I held out my hand. She took it and started to move. She hadn't lied: she really couldn't dance. Her body was too tense. She stood on my foot and apologised nervously.

'It's okay. Everything's okay.'

I guided her steps. My heart was pounding. Suddenly I felt that the whole reason I had spent all those years dancing was for this moment, in Isabelle's living room, so I could teach her, hold her tightly in my arms.

When we went to bed, she was tired and she said she'd rather we just went to sleep. That was perfectly fine with me. Even so, I feigned disappointment. Just a little bit, so she wouldn't think I wasn't attracted to her. And though I really did desire her presence, a hug was enough for me.

'I'm glad I met you,' she said. 'I don't know about you, but I feel quite alone here. I was transferred to this town a year ago, and all my friends live far away. And I never like the guys I meet on Tinder. They're too much like me – all they talk about, all they think about, is work. But you seem different. I like you.'

She fell asleep quickly. I was wide awake. It was too early for me, barely even one in the morning. So I spent a long time watching her in the darkness, my body lying against hers, her breath warm on my shoulder.

In the morning, she got up at seven. Still sleepy, I could vaguely hear her getting ready, making coffee. She sat on the edge of the bed.

'I have to go to work. But you can stay here and sleep a bit longer if you like. Just close the door when you leave.'

She thought for a moment, then said:

'Do you want to meet up tonight?'

'Okay.'

*

After that, without having to suggest that we 'start seeing each other' or some phrase like that, which I had always thought was obligatory for two people to become a couple, we simply became one, as if it wasn't even a question.

Our first weeks together went really well. I would meet Isabelle at her place after she had finished work. My shift ended earlier, so I would wait at home without doing anything in particular: some press-ups, some sit-ups, a bit of dancing on my rug, as if I was getting ready to go to The Beach, the absence of which no longer weighed heavily upon me. I could think about it without any kind of ache, just a serene excitement at the idea of taking Isabelle there when it reopened. At night, I would meet her at her apartment, where she would collapse exhausted onto the sofa without taking off her jacket. I sat next to her, feeling full of energy – my day was just starting. She told me about her day, complaining about her colleagues, her boss. I couldn't think of much to say to console her, so I just agreed with everything she said. When it was my turn to talk, it didn't last long because I had nothing to tell her. My days contained nothing but Isabelle. I preferred to listen to her, then do simple things together: watching TV, going to the supermarket, cooking, spending each evening like it was a little Sunday. And on Sundays, we would go for a walk in her neighbourhood. I felt good. I had achieved my goal. I was so happy that I didn't even think beyond that. The idea of introducing her to my parents or going on holiday together or starting a family . . . all of these grand dreams were far from my thoughts. Not being alone anymore . . . that was enough for me.

*

And then the big moment arrived: The Beach reopened. That night, we got ready together in my apartment. I felt a level of joy I had never experienced before, and it wasn't only because I was going to show the club to Isabelle. For the first time in my life, I would be going there without searching for anything, simply to enjoy what I already had. It must have been like a footballer playing a match when his team has already qualified for the tournament. While Isabelle took a shower, I put on Pharrell Williams's 'Happy' – the song of the year – and danced in the living room. After I'd showered, I kissed her and we made love, both of us still wet, as if the rest of the world could wait. I was careful not to let my head touch the sheets because I didn't want to mess up my hair. After sex, we got dressed and a peaceful atmosphere spread through the room: it was done, we were satiated, freed from desire, and now we had the whole night ahead of us for dancing and fun.

I knew the way there by heart: the succession of bends, the rhythm of the traffic lights. I could have walked there with my eyes closed, navigating my way solely from the sound of cars and the scent of trees. Walking with Isabelle, though, I realised that I had never really taken the time to look around. I'd been in too much of a rush, head lowered. Now everything was so beautiful: the passers-by, the shop signs, the pink sun setting over rooftops, all of it smiling down at us, accompanying us to The Beach, a cool breeze at our backs. As we got closer, it was as if the pedestrians around us were being filtered, and by the time we reached the docks, it was clear that everyone was headed to the same place. The night

started here, in this collective flow, the joy visible on the faces
of strangers, all of us converging on the nightclub.

Once we had crossed the bridge, I noticed people looking
at us. We were beautiful, Isabelle in an off-white Cos dress,
me in my black Uniqlo V-neck and my Levi's 501s. We walked
up to the entrance. There was a big crowd there for the reo-
pening; The Beach was back in business. I felt as pleased as if
I owned the club myself. As we stood in line, Isabelle asked
me questions: what kind of music they played, my favourite
drinks, the best spots on the dancefloor ... I had an answer
for everything. Suddenly I loved talking. I could have done it
for hours. She seemed thrilled by this.

Balou was the bouncer that night. He was one of my favour-
ites, a real force of nature – one night, I had seen him shove
an unruly client out of the club with his belly. I don't know
what got into me, but when I found myself next to him, I gave
him a hug, as if he were an old friend. He patted me on the
shoulder, looking embarrassed. I introduced him to Isabelle.
I wanted her to meet everyone I knew and even the people I
didn't know; I wanted them all to see us, for our happiness to
be widely understood.

Macklemore & Ryan Lewis – 'Thrift Shop'

During the three weeks of renovation, they had built a cir-
cular mezzanine, offering a perfect view of the dancefloor. It
was magnificent. Moving, even. Like a huge cathedral.

'So what do you think?' I asked Isabelle proudly.

Her face looked even prettier here, in the lights. She smiled
as she stared down at the dancefloor. Then she started laughing. I felt suddenly afraid.

'What? Don't you like it?'

'I love it! It's just so strange being here. I feel like I'm eighteen again!'

'Why eighteen?'

'No, I just mean ... it's so long since I've been to a nightclub!'

She kissed me.

'So what do you want to do first?'

'I'm going to introduce you to the best barmaid in the world!'

I felt like I was floating as I took her by the hand and led her through the crowd. On the way there, we stopped to pose for an official Soon Night photograph. I had always dreamed of doing that with my girlfriend. She placed her hand shyly on my shoulder and I put my arm around her waist and gave a thumbs-up.

'Say cheese!'

Alicia stood behind the bar. Unchanged, eternal. I had missed her too. I hugged her across the counter.

'Alicia, Isabelle. Isabelle, Alicia!'

Alicia held out her hand for a fist-bump, then discreetly winked at me, as if to say: 'I approve'. I felt blissful. Isabelle, Alicia, the entire nightclub ... I had absolute trust in all of it. I was in my element.

'Can we get two whisky and cokes?'

'On the house!'

Isabelle and I clinked glasses, facing each other on our barstools.

'To The Beach!' I said spontaneously.

'And to the two of us!'

'Yes, of course. To the two of us!'

The drink was delicious, perfectly mixed. Isabelle downed hers quickly and ordered another. She was no lightweight, I thought admiringly. As we drank, we watched the dancefloor and I started analysing the people out there: the good and bad dancers, the champions, the wallflowers, the drunks and the druggies, the boring ones, the lonely ones. I tapped my foot. I was itching to dance. Three weeks without it. That was a record for me. I felt sure it would be like getting back on a bike. Isabelle saw my eagerness.

'Shall we go for it? I'm a bit tipsy. I feel good.'

Pharrell Williams – 'Happy'

Dancing with Isabelle was the most intense and most natural thing I had ever done. Technically she wasn't brilliant, but that would come, I thought. The essential thing was this: facing her on the dancefloor, I could give her everything – words, caresses. Everything that I usually messed up or found awkward ... when I was here, it came out smoothly, converted into movements. There was no gap between what I felt in my heart and what my body expressed. I was myself. If I could have frozen my life in that moment, I would gladly have done it.

After a while, she put her mouth to my ear.

'I'm starting to get tired. I'd kind of like to go home.'

'Really? Already?'

'Yeah, it's almost three in the morning!'

I hadn't noticed the time passing.

'Could we please stay a bit longer?'

'Sure, if you like. But let's sit down, because my legs are on fire!'

I agreed to take a break in the mezzanine. Up there, the

atmosphere was pleasant, if a little too calm for me: some tables, a small bar, a general feeling of inertia. I ordered another whisky and coke; Isabelle got a glass of water. Our table was beside the railing, and I couldn't help looking down at the dancefloor below. For Isabelle, it must have been like I was staring at my phone. She touched my arm.

'You know, while we were dancing, I was thinking that maybe we could do something together next weekend. I could take the Monday off, so we'd have three days . . . I was thinking of Lisbon! We could rent an Airbnb. I'm friends with a couple who live there, so they could show us the less touristy parts of the city. It'd be great, don't you think?'

Taken aback, I shot her a tense little smile. I never left town, except to celebrate Christmas in Rennes with my brother and Audrey. The thought of Lisbon brought back sudden memories – of school trips, camping holidays, feelings of disorientation, endless days in the sun – and I broke out in a cold sweat. I wasn't ready to give up my habits.

'Um, I don't know . . . It's kind of expensive, isn't it, Lisbon?'

'Not especially. And we can come to an arrangement, if it's complicated for you. I don't mind at all.'

I must have had a constipated look on my face, impossible to hide, as when you're given a present that you don't like. I continued to stare down nervously at the dancefloor. She snapped her fingers to get me to look at her again.

'If you don't want to go to Lisbon, we could go somewhere else . . . I don't know, Barcelona, Naples . . . or even somewhere in France, like Marseille? It doesn't really matter. I just want us to do something together!'

To *do something*, she'd said, as if we hadn't done anything together yet.

'But we already do things, don't we?'

'I mean real things. Stuff that will get us out of our daily routine, help us get to know each other better . . . It just seems obvious to me.'

I was starting to feel uneasy. Her voice had changed, become more tense. Maybe because of the alcohol, I thought hopefully.

Without weighing my words, I said: 'I saw some flyers on the bar. Next Friday they're doing a nineties night here – that could be cool, don't you think?'

I regretted this instantly. She put a hand to her forehead, as though I was giving her a migraine.

'Listen, it was fun coming here tonight, but I don't plan on spending all my weekends here, nor my holidays. It's like you don't want to do anything else with your life, and that's freaking me out a little bit . . . Actually, now I think about it, I know hardly anything about you. That's not normal.'

In a flash, the three weeks that we had spent together shrunk and withered in my memory, making me feel ashamed. She kept talking, the words spilling out in a flood, as if everything she was saying had been on her mind for a long time.

'What do you expect from a relationship? I need you to tell me.'

'I don't know . . . It's hard to say . . . I'm fine with this . . .'

'You're satisfied with this?'

I didn't dare say yes, because I knew she wouldn't like

it, and yet that was very much what I thought. It seemed so simple to me: yes, I was satisfied with what we had. I was happy. I didn't want anything more from life than just being with her, the two of us close together, holding each other tight, with no need to move or speak ... Slowly, head lowered, I moved towards her, to take her in my arms, but she pulled back.

'Maybe it would be better if we ended this now.'

'Okay, I'll go to Lisbon!' I blurted out in a panic.

My heart was pounding, and I was staring into her eyes. On her face I saw, superimposed, the vague image of a foreign city, the sky, broad avenues packed with tourists, everything I was willing to brave for the chance to keep being her boyfriend.

But she just looked even more sorrowful.

'Arthur, it's okay, just let it go. I should have admitted the truth to myself before. At first I thought this might work. I thought you were different ... But it's not going to happen. We don't live on the same planet. We'd be bad for each other. I'm sorry.'

She was right. I felt the weight of that truth crushing me. All my thoughts converged painfully on the photograph of the two of us on the dancefloor, which would go online the next day. I didn't move. I was numb. There were tears behind my eyes.

'I'm going to leave now.'

She stood up, looking tired. I had the impression she was grappling with her sudden inability to feel moved, to empathise with me. But it was no longer her problem. She left.

I watched her walk away, disappear downstairs. Leaning over the railing, I tried to spot her below, but she must have been walking along the walls. All I could see now was the crowd on the dancefloor. I knew what I had to do. I had done it before. I needed to dive into that mass of bodies, to sink into it like a hot bath, let it dissolve every aspect of the last few weeks until nothing remained: neither the heartache nor the love.

ANGE

2017

That night, I danced for a long time with a woman in leggings and a baggy sweatshirt, who moved so impressively that I thought she must be a breakdancer. Her face tensed in concentration, her whole body spinning, she was standing one moment, dropping to the floor the next, forcing me to follow her out of my comfort zone. My heart was racing with joy and breathlessness. Finally she slowed down and, putting her hands behind my neck, kissed me. I fell into her embrace, eyes closed, and let her guide me. Nothing was ever as good as it was in those moments. Then she yelled into my ear, revealing her voice to me at the same time:

'You wanna get out of here?'

I checked my phone. Quarter to three. Fair enough.

'Okay!'

She took my hand and I followed her to the exit.

'Your place or mine?' she asked.

'Um, I don't know … yours?'

'Okay! What's your name, by the way?'

'Arthur. And you?'

'Mélissa!'

She smiled at me as she pushed open the door to the corridor that led outside. That was when it hit me: a slight head rush, a sort of déjà-vu feeling. Yes, I knew what would happen next. I knew it by heart: the cloakroom, the car park, the walk or taxi back into town, an unfamiliar apartment, one last drink, then sex, my mind already filled with fears about the next day, the shame I would feel when I looked in the mirror. Since breaking up with Isabelle about three years ago, all my failures had followed the same pattern: brief affairs – one night, two nights, sometimes a few more – that triggered fleeting, unconvincing visions of a future together, visions that suffocated and died in the cold air of reality, like a fish out of water. Away from the club, I never succeeded at anything. I tried so hard to play along, to make an effort, but all I got was a string of disappointments. And each time, I felt a growing weariness, the desire to give up. This time, suddenly, was one time too many. What was the point of getting hurt again? I'd be better off just going back to the dancefloor, enjoying the night until the very end.

'Actually, I think I'm going to stay.'

'What?'

She stared at me, uncomprehending.

'You seem a bit stressed ... Is it because you're not single? Well, don't worry – I've got a boyfriend too.'

'It's not that ... I'll only disappoint you.'

'You're kidding! Didn't you see how good we were together on the dancefloor? Come on, let's go!'

She grabbed my hand again. There was a look in her eyes that made my heart contract: a mix of desire and distress. For an instant, I imagined her life, her loneliness so close to mine, and the encounter that awaited us. I almost agreed to give it one last try, but something in me refused to yield: no, I didn't want this anymore. I was too scared. I couldn't stand the idea of getting my hopes up before disappointing her and losing her. For me to follow her, to believe that this could work, there would have had to be a tunnel under The Beach, an extension of the corridor that led from the dancefloor, packed with people, filled with music and movement, a long and possibly endless tunnel.

'Sorry.'

Her eyes went cold.

'You're weird. You could have warned me at least. Then I wouldn't have spent three hours dancing with you for nothing.'

And she went back inside, like someone going back to work, cleaving her way doggedly through the crowd. I waited a few minutes, feeling guilty, then went back myself.

I went to the bar to catch my breath. Seeing me coming, Alicia pushed a glass of water towards me. I had given up alcohol, and cigarettes too. The hangovers had started making my job unbearable.

'I thought you went off with the chick in leggings?'

'Yeah, I changed my mind.'

'You didn't like her?'

'I did ... A lot, actually, but ... I don't know ... I just felt like staying here.'

'Poor girl. You really got her hot as well . . .'

I smiled along, but I felt sad. I thought about Mélissa, and about all the others. Deep down, they all dreamed of leaving this place. For them, The Beach was merely a hunting ground, a passing phase. All you had to do was watch them. Most of them didn't care about dancing – you could see it in their eyes, their hurried movements. All they wanted was to find some-body and drag him out of there. In their desperation to find satisfaction, they were never able to enjoy themselves, rushing through the night to its desired destination, the bed, where they could rid themselves of their lust. I wished that I could keep them here, that the night would never end. I wished a ring of lava or fog would surround the club, forcing us all to live our lives here, sleeping on the leather benches, staying here forever. I thought about the videos of rave parties I had seen sometimes on YouTube, with thousands of figures turned to the wall of speakers, moving in a trance, unhurried, with no destination in mind, nothing but the pure joy of being there. I wondered if I would like that better than this. But I loved The Beach too much. I forgave my club its flaws, as if it were an old friend.

Scanning the floor in search of a new partner, I did not spot any good dancers. That was often the problem on the first few nights of the week. On Mondays, Tuesdays and Wednesdays, people came in smaller numbers and with less energy, and the overall level suffered as a result. You had to wait for Thursday for the dancefloor to catch fire. All the same, I did finally spot an unusual gathering in the middle of the floor, where a circle had formed around a man in dark glasses. He was a big man in every sense, with the body of an athlete past his prime – the beginnings of a belly, drooping pecs, male pattern baldness concealed by a completely shaved head – and yet he danced like a pro, alone in his Michael Jackson-like magnificence, an icon of pure, peerless dance.

I turned to Alicia. 'Do you know who that is – the guy in glasses over there?'

'No, he's a newbie! Good, isn't he? I bet you want to dance with him!'

I shook my head. He intimidated me. And he was a man, and men never let another man dance with them. I had tried a few times, and they'd always pushed me away in a sort of disgusted panic. Men dancing together here was simply impossible. Even women dancing with women was rare; I would see them sharing the occasional brief moment of complicity, but every time they would laugh knowingly and go back to dancing with men, as if it was just common sense. It was a waste, I thought, caused by a lack of curiosity. Everyone was automatically deprived of half their potential dance partners. Sometimes I found people here a little narrow-minded.

'Come on, it's obvious you want to! Go ahead! Have a dance-off with him! You two are the best dancers in the club! I really want to see this! I know you, Arthur – you'll regret it if you don't give it a go!'

I stood up. She was right. Who cared if he rejected me? I was dying to dance with him. I was dying to dance with the whole world.

Luis Fonsi –'Despacito'

Swaying to the rhythm, I headed back towards the centre of the dancefloor, pushed my way through the circle around

the man, and began to dance with him. To my surprise, he
wasn't hostile. In fact, he seemed galvanised by my presence,
whirling around and snapping his fingers. The circle closed
around the two of us. Some people shouted 'Dance-off!' and
I gave it all I had, moving my whole body, from my hair to
my toes. I didn't know his moves, he didn't know mine, and
our joint efforts to understand each other produced a sort of
fluid cement that soon spread among the others. Caught up
in our rhythm, they all came together to create a single giant
body, and for a few minutes I felt as if I was holding the entire
club in my arms. It was like the most intense orgasm I'd ever
experienced.

The song ended, a slower track came on, and everybody
started clapping and cheering. The man gave a low bow, then
gestured towards me, like an actor in a theatre. I bowed too,
blushing radiantly. He put his mouth to my ear.

'My name's Ange. You?'

He smelled of chemical mouthwash.

'Arthur!'

'*Enchanté*, Arthur!'

'*Enchanté!*'

I really was enchanted: this must have been the first time I
had used that expression without thinking how exaggerated
it seemed. A woman asked if she could take our picture.
Ange put his arm around my shoulders, pointing at the
camera with his hands making the shape of two revolvers.
I made the same pose, smiling so proudly that my lips were
practically touching my ears. I must have looked the same
way I used to look in school photographs when I managed to

sit next to the most popular boys, even though they weren't my friends. Ange could be my friend, though. He could be my main man, my dance partner not only for tonight but for other nights to come. Now I thought about it, I couldn't ask for anything more.

Just then, someone shoved Ange. Several people started booing him. Something must have happened, something I hadn't seen. The happy atmosphere suddenly evaporated. He stopped dancing. It was hard to tell what he was thinking behind those dark glasses. He gave the finger to a few people, then started walking away. I didn't have time to react. As he went past, he grabbed hold of my arm as though I was his child.

'I'll buy you a drink, comrade! We need to talk!'

Surprised, I let him lead me away. We went across the dancefloor and up the stairs to the mezzanine. He pointed to a table.

'Take a seat. I'll get the drinks. What do you want?'

'I ... I don't drink,' I stammered.

'Oh wow, you're a real purist. I love it! Back in a second, I'm going to get a whisky. That stuff fucks up your liver, but a man's gotta live, right?'

He set off like a rocket towards the bar. I took a breath and looked around. I hadn't been back to the mezzanine since my break-up with Isabelle. I could recall every detail: the table where we sat, the lighting, the volume of the music. For me, the entire floor remained sullied by that memory. I couldn't stand it. I would have gone straight back downstairs if not for Ange. I hadn't understood his anger, but I did remember him calling me comrade. *We need to talk, comrade.* Maybe he had an offer to make me? I hoped it would be another dance-off, maybe even several of them, if he started coming here regularly.

He returned with his whisky.

'So you've had it with women too?'

I was so taken aback, I couldn't think of anything to say.

'I've watched you dance. It's so unfair – you're good, man! You've got it all, it's obvious, and yet you're too scared to try anything ... Almost like you've lost the urge, right? I'm the same. You and me, we're in the same boat. It's become impossible to pull a girl normally. You saw that, right? I touch some girl's arse and everyone goes mental. But what's the big deal about touching some girl's arse?'

I didn't even feel annoyed. I was just disappointed, and a little bit repulsed. Ange sniffed as he waited for me to answer, then rubbed his thumb against his nose, which was probably full of cocaine. I didn't want to get into an argument, so I just shrugged. He nodded very seriously.

'Are you holding up okay?'

'Um ... yeah, I'm fine.'

'You don't let it get you down too much?'

'Um ... no, I'm fine.'

'You're right. Gotta keep fighting ... I swear, though, man ... These are sad times. Sad times, man.'

No matter what I said, he seemed to take it for granted that I agreed with him, that I shared his grievances. His *comrade* was the code word of a frustrated man. He didn't care about dancing. Sipping his whisky, he looked around bitterly, and the way he kept shaking his head and leaning towards me implicated me in his foul mood, as if he was behaving this way for both of us, in our joint name, as if we were on the same page. He took off his glasses and wiped them on his shirt. I was surprised by his eyes, which were small and dull, the eyes of a tired man.

'You know ... Sometimes I think we've got too old, that we're has-beens, that this is a generational problem. How old are you?'

'Thirty-seven.'

'There you go. That's old for a place like this. I'm forty, so you can imagine ... Fuck, man, we're has-beens! And it's the same everywhere, believe me. I just got back from a trip. I went clubbing all over Europe: Razzmatazz, Berghain, Egg, Privilege ... Everywhere you go, it's the same puritan bullshit. So maybe we should just forget it. Resign ourselves, you know. Stop going on the pull and getting humiliated. Move on to something else ...'

I nodded at these last words, hoping that he would suggest we head back to the dancefloor, that he would become again the Ange I had seen dancing. He leaned towards me and said solemnly: 'Comrade, I reckon we should team up.'

'Sure, I'd love that. I mean, I'm sure we're the best in the club.'

'That's what I think too.'

'So shall we go back?' I suggested enthusiastically.

'Not yet. First ...'

He rummaged with one hand in his trouser pocket. He took out a small vial of colourless liquid, which he showed me discreetly.

'You know what this is?'

I shook my head, feeling suddenly stressed.

'It's something you can put in a girl's drink, as a last resort. It makes them a bit more easy-going, if you see what I mean. It's better if you work as a pair, though. You and me.'

I panicked as I realised that he was talking about GHB. Alicia had told me about it once, about the terrible things that happened because of it. Forgetting everything else, I felt a sense of duty take hold of me, a stubborn residue of common sense and morality.

'Okay, but I need to go to the bathroom first,' I said, before adding: 'To piss.'

He stared at me and I worried that he was frowning suspiciously behind those dark glasses.

'All right. Be quick. I'll wait for you here.'

I went downstairs, too frightened to look back. I felt dirty, almost guilty. No, he didn't suspect anything, I told myself. He was waiting calmly as if it had never even crossed his mind that I might disapprove of his behaviour or betray him, as if he and I were identical. As soon as I was out of his sight, I headed straight to the bar. My mouth was dry and I was sweating.

In a rush of words, I told Alicia: 'That guy in the black glasses wants to drug a girl with GHB!'

Before she had time to react, I went out onto the floor and started dancing without thinking, while I waited for things to happen. Two or three songs were played. In all the movements around me, I could sense only latent violence, rage and frustration, the base urge to have sex or commit a crime.

It took up way too much space. It ruined the atmosphere. It was a darker version of the feeling I'd had in early adolescence, when I was about fourteen and my friends at school had given up having a laugh in the playground, preferring to think about girls, to talk about girls, to lust after them with all the force that they had previously put into other activities, becoming over-serious, obsessive, estranged from childhood, and tough shit for me if I wanted to keep running around or playing hide-and-seek during break time.

From the centre of the dancefloor, I watched two bouncers going up the stairs to the mezzanine, then speaking to Ange. He stood up, looking irritated. They grabbed his arm and led him away. While they were taking him to the exit, I kept dancing, head down. After a while, I looked up again. No sign of those black glasses anywhere. It was over: Ange had been removed. I tried to convince myself that this was good news, a bullet dodged. But all I felt was shame – and sadness. I had lost my best dance partner. He would never return to The Beach. I would never see him again.

It wasn't very late but the club was already starting to empty out. Keen not to waste any more time, I focused on my movements. In less than an hour there would be hardly anyone left in here: only the drunkest and most drugged-up would remain, the desperate ones, the ones who'd fallen asleep in the booths. I needed to make the most of what was left of the night, drink it down to the dregs.

Drake – 'Hotline Bling'

I woke up. It was past noon. My shift would start soon. My head felt hot, my legs sore. My mornings after were getting more and more difficult, even without alcohol. They were piling up on top of each other. I moved in my bed and smelled my rank breath on the pillow. My belly was bloated. I farted under the duvet, and a foul smell filled the room. How could I possibly have woken up this morning next to another body? Mine alone was too much to bear. I got up. I swallowed three Tylenol with a big glass of water. The dirty dishes stacked inside the sink stank of tinned tuna and scrambled eggs. There were bills on the chest of drawers – electricity, insurance, social security – that I was too afraid to open or throw away. On my phone screen, a message appeared from my mother, asking me if I was okay. Since retiring, my parents had been trying to improve their relationship with me. I answered immediately: *I'm fine, thanks. Love you both.* I had figured out a way to see them as little as possible, to avoid their judgement. I just needed to show them a bit of attention from time to time. Since they were used to not hearing from me at all, they were satisfied with even the smallest responses: a smiley face, an impromptu message, a brief conversation on Christmas Eve or a birthday was enough to reassure them, to fill their hearts and buy myself several weeks of peace.

I went out without bothering to wash. I was in a bad mood after my wasted night. Outside, the sun was shining down vertically on the town – no shadows, no subtlety, like an overlit mirrorball. Pollen floated through the heavy air and the trees were wearing too much scent. Everywhere I looked, people were on their lunch-break: in queues for bakeries, on restaurant terraces, on benches, in groups, alone on their phones. They all had a morning of life behind them. Now they were happily relaxing. Some of them looked up as I passed, my hair a mess, unwashed and unshaven, wearing an old, stained tracksuit. They reminded me of my father, when I was a child, returning from his run on a Sunday morning to find my brother and me still in bed, and gently reproaching us for our laziness before stretching out on the living-room sofa to make clear to us that he had already jogged seven miles that morning, as if that made any difference to us. For me, these people were the ones who were out of sync, out of step with reality. I didn't even look at them as I walked past, trying to look calm but trembling inside like a cornered deer. To me, these people were not people. They were fields seen through the windows of a train; they were fence posts, cars, obstacles littering the streets of this town that I had to cross to get to work.

On the high street, I passed McDonald's. The smell of the food made me hungry all of a sudden. I had time. I did sometimes cheat on my diet when my kitchen cupboards were empty. Burgers, kebabs, pizzas ... I had never lost the taste for these pleasures. They were pretty much all I had, beyond the confines of The Beach. *Who cares about having a six-pack, anyway?* I thought. It was only ever visible when I was naked, and by this point my one-night stands had slowed to a trickle. The main thing was to stay bulky so I looked good on the dancefloor. I went inside.

The touchscreens were all busy, so I had to order at the counter. Glancing up at the cashier, I thought I must be dreaming: it was Ange, wearing an apron and a McDonald's cap but no sunglasses. He had dark rings under his eyes, particularly his right eye. It might have been a black eye, in fact. I wanted to flee, but it was too late. Ange was waiting to take my order. He looked weirdly impassive, as though he didn't recognise me, but I couldn't believe that. The presence of his boss, just behind him, must have been curbing his anger. I could have tried bluffing him – smiling at him warmly and asking where he'd got to last night – but instead I panicked and decided to pretend that I didn't recognise him either.

'Um, a Maxi Best Of menu, CBO, fries and a Coke Zero,' I said, my voice rusty.

'For here or to take away?'

If I ordered it to take away, I might sound guilty.

'For here,' I answered firmly.

I paid.

'Take a seat. We'll bring your food out to you.'

I sat in the middle of the room, where I was clearly visible, trying to look unconcerned and innocent. I would have whistled if I'd known how. Sweat was pouring down my back.

Three minutes later, Ange himself brought my tray over.

'Enjoy your meal.'

He walked away without a backward glance. If he'd wanted to slip me a word, a threat or something worse, he'd missed his opportunity. For an instant I thought that maybe he really hadn't recognised me, having been too drunk last night, and I started to eat. But when I opened the box containing my burger, there appeared to be a gob of spit on top of the bun, right in the middle. I shuddered. Without moving my head, I peeked up at the counter: Ange was staring at me. I looked down. I didn't know what to do. That gob of spit seemed to weigh a ton. The mere sight of it made my heart race. Even so, I forced myself to eat my fries, drink my Coke and nibble around the edges of my burger, leaving the centre in the box like an apple core.

I didn't dare look at Ange again, nor leave for Bodymax, because what if he followed me? So I stayed where I was. A dribble of acid remained inside my throat. I felt heavy-limbed and ready to vomit, whether from the grease or the humiliation I wasn't sure. The restaurant emitted a sickening stench of sugary plastic. The heat of the sun was beating on my back through the windows, and sweat was stinging my skin. Voices called out order numbers. Sitting at tables in many different colours, the people around me ate their food: groups of hungover friends, loners like me, all of them in a rush, their fingers salty, as distant from me as the dead. I felt numbed by a dense, futile sadness. I wished I could disappear or fall asleep or teleport somewhere else, the way I used to in my daydreams as a kid. Minutes passed. I was late for work. Fuck it. I didn't want to go there anymore. I didn't want to go anywhere at all in the daytime. I'd call them or something to say I was quitting. I should have done it ages ago, in truth: stopped getting up in the mornings, given up dealing with all this shit, just slept all day, told the sun to fuck off, turned it inside out like a glove.

ALICIA

2018

One day Alicia told me she was quitting her job at The Beach. She was thirty-five and she wanted to find something *more real*. She had worked there full-time for seven years, a record. The other bartenders never stayed more than two years; they were often students, seasonal workers. Alicia suffered from insomnia and for a long time the nocturnal rhythm had suited her, but now all that was over. She was going to Angers to start a tapas bar with her chef boyfriend.

On her last night she brought him to the club – Carlos, a reserved man who did not go out much – then invited all the regulars to have a drink at the bar. I joined them with a heavy heart, sitting quietly on my bar stool. Unlike the others, I couldn't bring myself to celebrate her departure, to transform my sadness into happy nostalgia. Alicia was part of the furniture at The Beach. I couldn't imagine the place without her. She was as immutable as the palm tree, the concrete walls. This was an earthquake, but the others just laughed like a bunch of spongers at a leaving-do for some insignificant colleague. There were about ten of them, all men in their late thirties and early forties, none of whom I really knew, and who did not seem to know each other very well either; just a group of old loners who came here to hang out a few nights each week – often on Mondays and Tuesdays, when all the bars in town closed at midnight – to lean on the counter and tap their feet, or sway vaguely at the edge of dancefloor. I found them depressing. They weren't the only old people to come to the club, but the others always seemed to turn up for special occasions: groups of colleagues on an after-work outing; middle-aged couples commemorating their adolescence with a nostalgia-themed night; stag dos and hen parties; men in suits sitting in the VIP boxes. There was something bleaker about the regulars. I didn't want to be like them. After all, I was almost thirty-nine myself, more or less the same age as them. So I usually avoided them. When I danced, when I melted into the crowd, I still looked young. That was the advantage of being a late developer: I had hit puberty long after most of my contemporaries, struggling to become what is called a man. For a long time I had remained a child, then I'd been a 'young man' – because of my fine features, my hairless chin, my shyness – and now I was 'young for my age'; what had long been a source of embarrassment was finally transformed into an asset. Plus I looked after myself. Since becoming unemployed, I'd had full days to rest up for my evenings. I didn't go to the gym anymore, but I still worked out on a mat at home. My lifestyle was as healthy as an athlete's; the only difference was that I expended all my energy at night.

I spent a good hour waiting to find the right time to talk to Alicia, to tell her how much I would miss her, but she was too busy with the others, who insisted on paying for their drinks. I watched her and thought how great she was, in her yellow vest, with her sceptical smile, the way she could conduct three conversations at the same time, the way she slammed her shot glass on the counter after downing it. I didn't ever see her outside of The Beach; I had no idea what her life was like; I knew nothing about her hobbies or her secrets or her daily routines. After a while, I was torn from these thoughts when Fabrice, who I knew a little bit – an employee at a pizzeria, married, with a little girl – came over to see me, glassy-eyed.

'Hey, Arthur, pull my finger!'

I thought this was just a crude joke at first, then I noticed that he was holding out the wedding band on his ring finger.

'I've been trying to get this thing off for a while, but it's stuck. Maybe you can do it, with all your muscles!'

I gripped the ring and pulled, while Fabrice yanked his finger in the opposite direction, and the ring came free with a sound like a bottle being uncorked.

'All right! That's it, I'm asking for a divorce tomorrow, it's decided!'

'Stop it, Fabrice!' said Alicia. 'You've been saying that for six months! Nothing's decided at all. You love your wife!'

'This has nothing to do with love! Oh, forget it – I bet Arthur will understand where I'm coming from!'

Leaning on the bar stool next to mine, he turned to face me. I felt a sudden desire to escape to the dancefloor. I'd wasted enough time on this little party. I had the feeling that every moment I didn't spend dancing would be held against me, added to the tally of squandered days. The nights were short. Seven hours, on average. I hated it when they were frittered away like this. But politeness kept me glued to my bar stool, and I listened as Fabrice said:

'All right, long story short ... Valérie and I haven't had sex for two years ... Two bloody years! Would you be able to stand that, huh?'

I shrugged. He put his mouth close to my ear, and I smelled sweat and tequila.

'And listen, I'm not saying it's her fault. It's not mine either. It's the fault of time. Fucking time! We used to at least make an effort occasionally. Sometimes we'd even force ourselves. At least once a month, to keep up appearances, you know, and that was okay. But for the last two years ... nothing! It's like we've both given up. I swear, it's weird, but there's a sort of perverse pleasure in not doing it, like that's our only means of getting revenge on the other – depriving them of sex, because we don't feel like doing it ourselves. Do you see what I mean? But anyway, I've had enough – I'm getting a divorce tomorrow! Tomorrow morning! One of us has to take the initiative. We're still young – we can't just let ourselves die like this. Look at the dancefloor. All those people, I want to kiss them all! So, come on – tonight we dance!'

It was Alicia who rescued me.

She yelled drunkenly: 'I want to dance too!'

Leaving her co-worker to look after the bar, she walked out from behind the counter and joined us at the edge of the dancefloor. I had never seen her on this side of the bar before. She stood in front of me.

'And I'm going to start with John Travolta himself! I've always dreamed of this!'

She nimbly held out her hand, as if she was inviting me to the ball. The others whistled as I took her hand.

'Don't worry, Carlos!' one of them shouted. 'He's not going to steal her from you! He's the most chaste bloke in the whole club!'

They laughed as Alicia dragged me to the middle of the dancefloor.

Ariana Grande – '7 rings'

There were two ways of dancing to this track: either you kept time with the rapid, jerky rhythm of the words, or you followed the deep swell beneath. While the rest of the club went for the first option, we pressed our bodies together and slowed our cadence, isolated in a bubble of languor, as if we were dancing to a ballad. Alicia was a sentimental drunk; you could see it in her eyes. She wanted to tell me something intimate, intense. She moved her face close to mine so she wouldn't have to shout.

'You know, Arthur ... I'm going to miss you most of all. You were my favourite.'

Gratitude made me smile and stung my eyes as though I'd bitten into a lemon. I wanted to tell her sweet things too, to give her pleasure with my words, so she would carry them away in her memories.

'I'm going to miss you too. You're my best friend.'

For an instant she looked surprised, then she kissed my cheek.

'Do you realise how many nights we've spent together?'

I tried to count them in my head. There must have been more than a thousand.

'What will you do without me? Who'll serve you glasses of water? Nobody can do that as well as me.'

'Nobody ... I'll drink from the bathroom sink, I promise.'

She laughed. There was a silence. She appeared to hesitate.

'Seriously, though ... What are you going to do with your life? I mean, do you think you'll keep coming here much longer?'

'I don't know ... Yeah. Why?'

'I never told you this before because you were a client, but I can say it now. Sometimes I think you deserve better. I mean, not better, but ... *more.*'

She tried to find the right words, smiling with drunkenness and embarrassment, holding me delicately in her arms, as if to console me for the pain she was about to inflict.

'I don't know what you do when you're not here – during the daytime, I mean – because we've never talked about that. But I'm not naïve. I know people like you are unusual. And you're more extreme than the others ... I just feel like you're giving up on so many things. And I think someone as kind and gentle as you ... Sometimes it just bothers me that your whole life seems to be centred on this club. You could have so much more! You could find a job you like ... Fall in love ... Start a family ... Or go on a trip! Around the world, you know? I'd be so happy for you.'

She fell silent. Her eyes were glistening. She was waiting for me to react, but I didn't know what to say. I had lost the ability to think about things like that. They were too big. They made my heart pulse in my throat.

'I'm fine here,' I said simply.

She looked at me with sorrowful, tender eyes.

'You can't spend your whole life here ... Time passes ... You need other plans ... And you have to find a way to make money ... I mean, you can't just stay unemployed ... I was thinking about dancing, for instance ... You're a great dancer! You could do something with that ... I don't know, go to auditions, join a dance company, or teach other people how to dance, make a career of it ...'

I felt ill. She didn't understand. My life revolved around The Beach. Everything else was foggy, hostile. I was afraid of it all: the streets, having a job, paperwork, questions, unfamiliar faces seen in daylight. Something inside me was jammed. It was hard to explain. Maybe as difficult as when you can't dance, I thought. That must be the same problem, only in reverse. I had given up the fight. I knew that wasn't a good thing, but there was nothing I could do about it. I felt suddenly dizzy, as though I was standing on the edge of a tall building. I wanted this conversation to end.

'Please, can't we just dance? I just want to make the most of your last night. That's all that matters right now.'

She nodded, resigned, and closed her eyes. I held her more closely, gently laying my head in the hollow of her neck, and we danced like that until the song ended.

The DJ abruptly flipped the ambience, following up with Cardi B's 'Money', an aggressive rap song. Carlos, Fabrice and the others all joined us, jumping up and down. Alicia and

I moved apart, our eyes met for one last instant and then, amidst the laughter and flailing limbs, everything else disappeared, leaving nothing but the dance – and the manageable sadness of saying goodbye to a friend.

LÉO

2019

And finally there was this night in December 2019.

I woke up late in the afternoon. It was the worst moment of the day, when I was no longer tired enough to keep sleeping and yet I still had several hours to get through before I could go out again. I spent them like it was a Sunday, like I was a convalescent, moving sluggishly between the kitchen and my bed, masturbating without desire so I could scrape together a few more winks of sleep. I hated my apartment: its emptiness, its silence and the hum of the fridge, the lingering odour of something I couldn't identify . . . me, maybe. After a while, I opened the window to look outside. There were lots of people in the streets. It would be Christmas soon. In the distance I could see the lights lining the high street. I remembered the smells of churros and mulled wine. I felt a bit sad, so I closed the window. What did I have to complain about, after all? I had found my equilibrium, the only one worth anything: being alone intermittently, being happy

after nightfall. 'You can't have everything,' as my parents
had often told me.

As the hours passed and the daylight faded, I felt a tranquil
joy spread through me. I could feel it getting closer: the sound
of the bass, the crowd on the dancefloor, other bodies pressed
against mine. I took a shower. I didn't bother making my bed
or cleaning my apartment. I put on the last pair of clean boxers
in my drawer – the ugliest pair I had, beige check, the elastic
worn out, dating back to the time when my mother still used
to buy my clothes for me. What did it matter? Nobody would
see them anyway. I ate some crackers and a banana: no time
to cook. I closed the shutters so the sunlight wouldn't bother
me when I got home, then I went out.

I arrived in the car park at ten on the dot, freshly washed
and nicely dressed, just as the club was opening. Nobody
could have guessed what kind of day I'd had. Strangely, all
the people I saw in the queue were very young. Teenagers,
by the look of them. The style of their clothes, the sounds
of their voices and their laughter ... there was a disturbing
uniformity about it. I felt the same awkwardness I had felt
that first time, with Vincent and the others, surrounded by
people who were older than us. Once again, I stuck out like
a sore thumb, but this time I was the old guy, and everyone
was staring at me.

Ignoring them, I skipped the queue and headed straight towards the bouncer on the door. I liked doing this: not having
to wait, not having to be searched. It made me feel privileged.
Every night, I would see people turned away because they

were too drunk, too alone, gangs of men without women, troublemakers, repeat offenders, and sometimes the homeless guy from under the bridge who would go through the motions of trying to get in. All of them failed in their mission, were sent packing, back to the void, while the door was held open for me. My VIP pride was still tinged with fear, though. I always had the feeling that a hand might emerge from the queue to grab me by the collar and drag me back in line, as if I wasn't entirely convincing, as if a hint of overexcitement remained on my face.

'Hey, Mickaël, all good?'

'All good. You?'

'All good.'

A brief discussion, sticking to the essentials. Fake clubbers were easily recognisable from the way they would talk too much. The outside world had no place here. No conversations about work, or personal problems, or the weather. There was no weather at The Beach. It was an airtight box, a microclimate. I was about to go inside when Mickaël barred my way.

'Sorry, Arthur, it's Fresh Blood tonight . . .'

'Fresh Blood?'

'It's a special student night. The boss's idea. Didn't you see the Facebook page?'

I never went on Facebook anymore. There was nothing in my feed now apart from a few people I didn't remember who continued to wish me happy birthday every year and who would probably have kept doing it even if I was dead.

'Come back tomorrow.'

'I can't go in?'

'Well, technically, no. Because you're not a student.'

He continued to vet the people in the line. I stood to one side. I couldn't get my head around the idea of walking away. It was absurd. This wasn't a Sunday. I had to dance. I tried to think of arguments in my favour. I wasn't used to having to talk my way in, never mind getting into a fight about it, but I felt ready to go that far if necessary.

'I just want to dance . . . I'm not going to bother anyone.'

'I know, I know . . . And you really can't wait till tomorrow?'

'Well, it does kind of bother me . . . I never normally miss a night.'

He sighed. For the first time, I saw in his eyes – generally so cold and neutral – an ounce of compassion. I felt embarrassed.

'All right, since it's you, go ahead. But you're going to feel out of place, I'm warning you . . . You'd be better off waiting till tomorrow.'

My embarrassment faded.

'Don't worry, I'll be fine. Thanks.'

'I've never seen a guy as mad about dancing as you. You should be in the *Guinness World Records*.'

I went inside. I left my coat in the cloakroom. They didn't need to give me a token; I had my own hanger. Walking through the corridor, I breathed in that odour, so familiar and yet every time still so intense, as if I was discovering it for the first time: the smell of an underground car park, of imminence, the smell of a hidden world rumbling behind the black door.

The dancefloor was empty at this time of night. People were still arriving, and nobody dared go first. Things often didn't get moving until around midnight, depending how good the DJ was. Normally I would have jumped in straight away to get things going, but in the circumstances I decided to keep a low profile. I headed diagonally towards the bar. I hadn't been there since Alicia left. Her replacement, a somewhat snooty young man, was reluctant to serve me glasses of water if I wasn't going to buy anything, so I preferred to drink tap water from the bathroom. From the dancefloor to the toilets and back: that was my only axis of movement these days. All the rest – the mezzanine, the terrace, the smoking area, the VIP boxes – seemed generally pointless to me, not much different from places outside of The Beach, with their slowness and their impossible encounters.

Around eleven, the first people started dancing. I enjoyed observing that initial shyness, which would soon be forgotten, drowned in the heaving mass. I couldn't resist for long. Sliding across the floor as if on a moving walkway, I entered the dancefloor.

Aya Nakamura – 'Pookie'

I loved this song. I danced while lip-syncing the words with an expression of feigned outrage, my upper body fluid and my lower body jerking to the beat. This was always a success. I remembered how Alicia always used to criticise the latest music, saying it was too rap, not melodic enough, telling me how she thought music was better before. I didn't agree with that at all. I didn't feel like there had been any sudden change in style, more a gradual evolution. In the same way that my parents probably never noticed that their children were growing up since they saw them every day, for me music

was transforming imperceptibly. It never took me by surprise.
I didn't hear the time passing.

Little by little, the dancefloor started to fill up. A crowd
emerged. Tonight, it gave off a shared energy, like a really
great Saturday night. That was the Fresh Blood effect, I supposed. Everyone here was in their early twenties. I needed
to synchronise my movements to theirs if I wanted to fit in.
Confidently, I began holding out my hands, offering dances.
But it didn't work. After several attempts, I realised that the
same thing was happening every time: they were avoiding
me, not in a mean way, but automatically, the way you might
swerve past a telegraph pole while walking down the street.
They must have thought I was too old to dance with them.
I understood this: for some of them, I was probably close to
their father's age. And age, here, was unfortunately one of
the obstacles that divided people. I didn't panic. I decided
to change my strategy. Since nobody wanted to dance with
me as part of a couple, I would create a more general movement, bring together an entire group. To achieve that, I began
dancing more visibly: whirling my arms, jumping in the air,
spinning in a circle. I was like a tornado of moves ... But
things went from bad to worse. The better I danced, the more
the others distanced themselves from me. I felt like I was
wearing a huge inflatable rubber ring. Not only did nobody
join in with my rhythm, but some of them slowed down or
stopped dancing completely. I even saw two people filming
me with their mobiles, and they were laughing. I was starting to sweat. Hot, acrid sweat that stung my eyes. To save
my dignity, the only thing I could think to do was continue

dancing, with ever more vigour, ever more speed ... I tripped over – the sole of my right foot got stuck on my left ankle as I was trying to spin to the right on my left leg: a beginner's mistake – and I fell. I caught myself with one hand and felt my wrist crack. Instantly I jumped back up, and to avoid their looks I left the dancefloor, eyes down, cheeks burning. Through the wall of bodies I could see the booths at the back of the room, half-hidden in the shadows. I moved miserably towards them.

I didn't sit there very long. The leather was cold, the seat too low. The beams of light stopped at my feet. I was on the sidelines. The crowd had healed itself around my absence, and people were continuing to dance without me. My wrist throbbed. I didn't dare go back. They would only reject me again. Suddenly I was afraid of other people. It was horrible: I felt just as scared as if I'd been standing in a busy street in the middle of the day. The club was disfigured; I no longer recognised it. Loneliness hit me like a draught of cold air, as if someone had left a door open. For a second, I even thought about leaving.

It was just then, turning towards the exit, that I noted the presence of another person on the leather bench, sitting several feet away, looking equally alone. I was intrigued by him. He was a teenager in a New York baseball cap, hunched over his phone. He looked very young, maybe seventeen. He was skinny, face covered with acne, a bumfluff moustache. His shoulder blades stuck out under his T-shirt like a little kid's. His legs, in skin-tight jeans, were like stilts ending in a pair of enormous, brand new Nikes. A flash of light revealed tears in his eyes. I froze. I had never seen anyone cry here before. The mass of bodies on the dancefloor continued to move. Nobody came to help him. I felt a sudden urge to do something, although I didn't know what. Should I wave? Ask him if he was okay? Put a hand on his shoulder? All these ideas crossed my mind, but I didn't dare act on them. And then I remembered the pack of tissues in my pocket. I could give it to him so he could wipe his eyes.

I slid slowly across the bench towards him. He sensed my presence, glanced at me suspiciously, then sniffed and stared down at his phone screen again. I handed him the pack.

'Take this, if you want!'

He gave me another suspicious look, but he took the tissues anyway and blew his nose.

'Thanks,' he mumbled.

His voice sounded as though it was still in the process of breaking.

'You're welcome,' I said.

Then there was a long silence, during which I was probably expected to move away. But I didn't. I wanted to continue our conversation. He kept staring at his phone, his finger scrolling the screen, just for something to do. He clung to it. He reminded me of the teenagers I would sometimes see in the street, hanging out in a group, an earbud in one ear, listening to a conversation with the other, half-withdrawn, like a boxer turning his face sideways because it offered his opponent less to aim at. The tears were no longer rolling down his cheeks, but his eyes were red.

I tried to think of something to say. I had never been great at making conversation with strangers, but by now I was completely useless.

'Are you okay?'

'Yeah.'

'If you need anything, I can try to help you. I know this place really well.'

'Thanks, but I'm fine.'

At that moment, three boys – the same age as him, but much bigger – stood in front of us. At first they didn't realise I was with him.

'Léo, we've been looking everywhere for you! Come on, we found you one! She's got big tits too!'

He laughed nervously.

'Come on, let's go!'

'I'll come in a minute!'

'No, come now! Enough of this bullshit! Lads, drag him over! Otherwise he'll spend the whole fucking night here!'

Laughing, they began pulling him by the arm. He resisted. He was laughing too, but his face was tense, his hands tightly gripping the bench, and the little noises that came out of his mouth sounded more and more like wails of protest. Without thinking, I stood up.

'Leave him alone.'

The three boys stopped. My voice had shaken, but they obviously hadn't noticed because I saw fear in all their faces.

'Who's that? Léo, are you with him?'

They started laughing nervously again. They stared at the two of us, looking troubled, then backed away.

'We'll leave you to it, then . . .'

They went back into the crowd. Just before they vanished, I heard one of them say: 'Who's that old guy?'

'Hey, I'm coming!' Léo shouted, his voice mutating from a grunt to a squeak, his body leaning towards them as if he was trapped in slow motion.

I sat back down. There was a silence. Léo didn't dare look at me anymore. I felt equally bad for both of us.

'They're your friends?' I asked.

'Yeah.'

'And you don't want to go with them?'

He shrugged.

'I do.'

He looked at the dancefloor. The lights sparkled off his perfectly still face. His hands still digging into the leather, his torso still angled forward, he hesitated. Several memories bubbled confusedly to the surface of my mind. I saw myself as a child standing on the diving board above the municipal swimming pool, breathing the smell of chlorine, hearing the muffled echo of the water; I saw myself perched on some rocks during a holiday in Spain, wearing plastic sandals and looking down at my brother, in the river below, yelling at me to jump; and I saw myself here, twenty years ago, before I'd learned to dance, sitting at the edge of a group of friends in this very booth. Suddenly Léo started crying again. The tears came more violently this time, in sobs that shook his whole upper body. 'Fuck ... fuck ...' he kept saying, jaw clenched, ashamed of his own emotion. I didn't know what to do. I wanted to take him in my arms, but something held me back. I was so much older than him and we didn't know each other. It would have been too weird. And I think it was that unbridgeable chasm between this teenager and me that made me start crying too, softly. The tears took me by surprise, as if a dam had burst. I think that was the first time I'd wept since childhood. I didn't try to stop myself. I let the tears fall without really understanding why, sitting there motionless beside him. And the two of us stayed like that for quite a long time.

At last, Léo sniffed, shifted position and looked at me. His face was puffy, his lips were wet, and there was snot running over his bumfluff moustache, but I wasn't disgusted by his appearance. I felt the way I imagine someone might with a very close friend or relative.

'Sorry,' he said.

He didn't notice that I was crying too, maybe because of the lights. He scratched his head and glanced at the time on his phone. I was afraid he was going to leave. I had an idea to keep him here.

'If you like, I could teach you to dance. I'm pretty good at it. It might help you feel better here.'

He looked surprised. For an instant, I saw an expression of shy enthusiasm on his face and I thought he was going to say yes, but he shook his head.

'I'm going to go home. It's better that way. But thanks.'

He stood up. I didn't try to stop him. He looked unsure how to say goodbye to me. In the end he just smiled and waved, and I did the same. I felt a pleasant warmth near my heart. He walked away, along the wall. I watched his cap moving through the crowd until it disappeared.

I was tired. My head felt hot and heavy. The people on the

dancefloor were blurred by my tears, and they looked very distant. I told myself that I had done everything I could to get closer to those people, and to all the others, that I had tried really hard and I shouldn't blame myself for having failed. I shut my eyes so I wouldn't have to see anything anymore, and it must have been soon after that that I fell asleep.

ARTHUR

This Morning

I can no longer hear the clink of glasses. The barman must have finished washing them. Any moment now he will walk across the dancefloor and he'll spot me. He'll ask me to leave, and I will. I'll probably go home. I don't know what I'll do after that. I have the feeling that the walls of my apartment will close in on my bed, that the loneliness will crush me.

At the other end of the club, the door opens and a man enters. It's the boss. I've seen him here before, always from a distance – on the mezzanine, in the VIP boxes. I'm afraid that he'll get annoyed when he sees me and have me kicked out, so I pretend I'm still asleep. I hear him chatting with the barman for a minute. And then: 'What's that guy doing there, in the booth?'

'Oh, sorry, I didn't notice him.'

They come over. I keep my eyes tightly closed. The boss puts his hand on my shoulder.

'Hey, man ... Come on, look at me ... It's obvious you're just pretending to be asleep. It's okay, I'm not going to do anything bad to you ... Quite the opposite, in fact ... I know who you are ... My most faithful client ...'

I hesitate. Abruptly he shakes my shoulder and I open my eyes without meaning to.

'There you go!'

It's the first time I've seen him up close. He's in his sixties, with a pot belly, tired blue eyes, and very blond hair that looks almost yellow. Dyed, I realise: it's white at the roots. His cheeks look oddly rubbery and his face is frozen in a strangely emotionless smile. Suddenly I recognise him. His name is Guy. He's the one who slapped me the first time I came here.

'So what happened to you?'

I sit up groggily.

'Sorry.'

'Too much to drink last night?'

'He doesn't drink,' says the barman.

'So what's up, then? Somebody break your heart?'

I can't think of anything to say. I wish I was literally part of the furniture, that they would just leave me here.

'Anyway, I'm sorry but we're closed, so you're going to have to leave. But I'll take you for a drink if you like. There's a bar that opens early on the docks. It'll give us a chance to have a chat. I've been wondering about you for some time now.'

He holds out his hand, still smiling in the same way. He intimidates me as much as ever. I obey without thinking. My body is heavy. We walk across the dancefloor together. I don't recognise it anymore. It has a colour, I realise. Green-grey. It's sticky. The soles of our shoes make squelching noises. Scattered over it, I see coins, keys, bus tickets, tissues, a broken pair of glasses ... As we pass the bar, Guy runs a finger along it to see how dirty it is. He looks at the results and frowns.

'I was expecting more people.'

He keeps walking and I follow him. As we pass through the first door, I feel like I am observing the place more attentively, the way you do when you're really leaving.

In the corridor, two women are waiting with a cleaning trolley. I have never seen them before. It's never even crossed my mind until now that the club needs to be cleaned. And yet it's obvious, because we've been dancing here all night. Everything must be erased so that the next clients will find it as good as new, like a hotel room. So they won't think about the nights that came before. So they will experience their night as the only one.

Outside, the sky is already too light. The sun is making its presence felt behind the veil of clouds. The town is waking up. There is something cold and pitiless about mornings. They soak up the thickness of the night like ink. Usually I hurry home before dawn so I don't have to see too many people. A few workers, the bin lorry, the smell of warm bread ... This time, I walk slowly beside Guy, from the car park to the bridge then along the docks.

'I'm pleased to meet you. I've seen you dancing before. You really lift the atmosphere in the club. So where are you from? How long have you been coming here?'

I think about that birthday party. But I don't want to mention it, for fear that he will get embarrassed or angry, decide not to take me to the bar after all, leave me alone earlier than expected.

'Um . . . a long time.'

'I really like having some old regulars. There are fewer and fewer of you. So tell me, what is it you like about this club? Why are you so faithful to it? I'd like to know, obviously.'

'I don't know . . . I like meeting people.'

'And you're satisfied with the atmosphere, the quality?'

'Um . . . yeah, yeah.'

'And compared to previous years – like the nineties, the early two thousands – do you think it's changed much? Was it better before?'

'I don't know . . .'

'A little bit?'

'Maybe a little bit, yeah.'

He sighs, as if he's disappointed in me.

I try to make up for it. 'But it's still really good.'

'Don't be embarrassed – I agree with you. Of course it was better before.'

He thinks for a moment, then continues in a serious tone, as if getting something off his chest.

'I can tell you this in confidence . . . Things are getting tricky for us. We're losing money. Times have changed. Back then, everyone used to meet up in clubs. It was the norm. But now people prefer hanging out at home or going to concept bars or concerts. And then there are all these dating apps, social media, and so on . . . We can't get the numbers in. I'm doing my best. That's why I organised the Fresh Blood night, for instance, and there's other stuff like that, but the problem goes deeper. I mean, look around at all the clubs that are closing. Just this year, in this area, The Loft has closed . . . Pili-Pili has closed ... Millennium has closed ... and Ibiza doesn't have long left either. One day it'll be our turn. That's just how it is. Nothing lasts forever. It happened to village fêtes, to the old dance halls ... It'll happen to nightclubs too eventually. I give us another few years. Maybe five. Maybe less. You're never safe from a nasty surprise.'

Strangely, hearing this, I don't feel any sadder than before. As if my tiredness and The Beach's are the same. As if it is perfectly logical that the two of us should reach the end of our clubbing days at the same time. I even feel a certain relief.

'When that happens, I'll retire. I'll go south, to the Côte d'Azur. My daughter lives down there. It'll be fine.'

He looks at me.

'What about you? Where will you go when it's over?'

I try to think. He laughs then and pats my back, suddenly cheerful again.

'Don't worry, we're not there yet.'

The bar is called L'Escale. I have often walked past without noticing it. The shopfront is discreet: a floor-to-ceiling window, with thick beige curtains concealing the interior. Guy opens the door.

It's a small, poorly heated, old-fashioned bar. When you cross the threshold, the tarmac of the street changes abruptly to tiles, with no step or transition between the two. The ceiling lamps give off a bright white light. There's a zinc-topped bar, a few tables, a TV set showing sport, the murmur of a radio, and group photographs covering the walls. A dozen middle-aged men – the youngest ones in their forties, the eldest in their sixties – are sitting around drinking coffee, beer, wine. Having got up early, they look like they're already tired. Maybe they just haven't fully woken up yet.

'Hello, hello! I'd like to introduce you all to Arthur, our biggest fan. He holds the record for the most nights spent at The Beach. And he's a great dancer too.'

The men greet me, looking interested. One of them, sitting at the back, even starts to applaud.

'Yes, yes, a round of applause for Arthur!'

They all stand and clap then, as if I am a returning champion. I stand in the doorway, intimidated. Guy leads me over to the barstools.

'Hi, Sylvie.'

He kisses the barmaid on the cheeks. She's in her sixties, with long hair, wearing a skin-tight black top. There are little bulges of flesh on her belly and her hips. She has a pretty smile.

'I'll have a Kir, please. Arthur, what would you like?'

I don't dare ask for a glass of water, since he's invited me for a drink.

'Um, a whisky and coke please.'

'We're out of whisky, sorry.'

'Okay . . . Same thing, then.'

She puts our glasses on cardboard coasters. Guy raises his in the air.

'To The Beach.'

'To The Beach.'

We drink in silence. I was expecting Guy to have more to say, but instead he just stares into space. Several minutes pass like that. Then he finishes his drink, puts some money on the counter, and says: 'Arthur, I'm going home now.'

He gets up from his bar stool. I stand up too, but he gently pushes me back.

'Please, stay. I don't want to rush you. I've left enough money for you to have another drink – it's on me. And Sylvie will be nice to you, won't you Sylvie?'

'I'll try . . .'

I hesitate. It's true that I don't want to go home, but I am afraid of finding myself alone in this new place, with these people who I don't know.

'Okay,' I say, deciding to give it a try.

Guy shakes my hand.

'I'm glad I met you. Thanks for bringing my club to life. See you soon?'

I smile so I don't have to say yes. He leaves. When he opens the door, a beam of daylight enters, stretching all the way to the bar then retreating as soon as the door closes, returning the room to its artificial light.

All the men look at me and smile. They seem pleased that I have stayed here with them. I feel a little better. Flattered, even. Their bodies don't move, but there's an unusual gentleness to their faces. They seem approachable. I smile back at them and sip my drink.

'So,' says Sylvie, 'you're a great dancer?'

I blush.

'Apparently . . .'

'What kind of dancing do you do?'

'Depends on the song. I like a bit of everything.'

'Watch out,' one of the men says. 'She loves dancing too. Sometimes she tries to get us to join in ...'

Several men laugh. I try to think of something nice to say. 'I wouldn't mind that.'

'Ooh, the young 'un's up for it, Sylvie ...'

'I'll take you up on that,' says the barmaid.

She turns off the sound on the television and looks at her mobile phone. My heart is racing.

'What shall I put on? Something fairly easy. I'm a bit rusty ... Oh, I know!'

An old pop song comes on. I recognise it: 'I Wanna Dance With Somebody' by Whitney Houston. My parents used to listen to it sometimes when they were cooking dinner, I remember, and I would sit on the sofa, my feet dangling, and clap along. Sylvie comes around from behind the counter and holds out her arm as Whitney starts singing the chorus.

I hesitate before taking her hand. I've never danced in the morning before. It's worth a try, though. Why should dancing be restricted to certain hours, after all? I stand up and she leads me into the middle of the room. Her body is warm. It relaxes softly into mine. That's all. I'm fine. I'm not alone. You're never alone, when you're dancing with somebody.